THE SECOND SWORD

and

MY DAY IN THE OTHER LAND

FARRAR, STRAUS AND GIROUX NEW YORK

THE SECOND SWORD

A TALE
FROM THE
MERRY
MONTH OF
MAY

MY DAY IN THE OTHER LAND

A TALE
OF
DEMONS

PETER HANDKE

TRANSLATED FROM THE GERMAN BY
KRISHNA WINSTON

Farrar, Straus and Giroux
120 Broadway, New York 10271

The Second Sword copyright © 2020 by Suhrkamp Verlag,
Frankfurt am Main
My Day in the Other Land copyright © 2021 by Suhrkamp Verlag,
Frankfurt am Main
Translations copyright © 2024 by Krishna Winston
All rights reserved
Printed in the United States of America
The Second Sword was originally published in German in 2020 by
Suhrkamp Verlag, Germany, as *Das zweite Schwert*
My Day in the Other Land was originally published in German in
2021 by Suhrkamp Verlag, Germany, as *Mein Tag im anderen Land*
English translations published in the United States by
Farrar, Straus and Giroux
First American edition, 2024

Library of Congress Cataloging-in-Publication Data
Names: Handke, Peter, author. | Winston, Krishna, translator. |
  Handke, Peter. Zweite Schwert. English. | Handke, Peter.
  Mein Tag im anderen Land. English.
Title: The second sword : a tale from the merry month of May.
  My day in the other land : a tale of demons / Peter Handke ;
  translated from the German by Krishna Winston.
Other titles: My day in the other land
Description: First American edition. | New York : Farrar, Straus
  and Giroux, 2024.
Identifiers: LCCN 2023039177 | ISBN 9780374601447
  (hardcover)
Subjects: LCGFT: Novellas.
Classification: LCC PT2668.A5 S43 2024 | DDC 833/.914—
  dc23/eng/20230918
LC record available at https://lccn.loc.gov/2023039177

Our books may be purchased in bulk for promotional,
educational, or business use. Please contact your local
bookseller or the Macmillan Corporate and Premium Sales
Department at 1-800-221-7945, extension 5442, or by email at
MacmillanSpecialMarkets@macmillan.com.

www.fsgbooks.com
Follow us on social media at @fsgbooks

1   3   5   7   9   10   8   6   4   2

Contents

THE
SECOND
SWORD

A TALE
FROM THE
MERRY
MONTH OF
MAY

For Raimund Fellinger, in memoriam

Then said he unto them, But now, he that hath a purse, let him take it, and likewise his scrip: and he that hath no sword, let him sell his garment, and buy one . . . And they said, Lord, behold, here are two swords. And he said unto them, It is enough.

—LUKE 22:36–38

I

BELATED REVENGE

"So this is the face of an avenger!" I said to myself on the morning in question as I looked in the mirror before setting out. I mouthed this statement without a sound, yet articulated every word, moving my lips with exaggerated precision, as if to read those lips in the mirror and commit the formulation to memory, once and for all.

In the past I'd often talked to myself this way for days on end—and not just in the last few years—but at this particular moment I experienced the conversation as unprecedented for me, and also unheard-of—in every sense.

So this was how a human being spoke and looked who, after years of hesitating, procrastinating, and occasionally forgetting the whole thing, was about to leave the house and exact long overdue revenge, on his own behalf, true—perhaps—but beyond that for the sake of the world and in the name of a universal law, or also merely—why "merely"?—in order to shake up and thereby wake up a certain public. What public? The one that mattered.

The strange part was this: as I gazed at myself, the "avenger," in the mirror, seemingly the embodiment of calm and projecting an authority that transcended all others, and spent probably a good hour taking stock of my image, especially the eyes, almost unblinking, I felt my heart growing increasingly heavy, and once I'd left the mirror and my house and garden gate behind, it even ached.

My usual way of talking to myself, always quite loquacious, was often not only silent but also completely expressionless, going unnoticed by others—or at least so I imagined. At other times I shouted at the top of my lungs, alone in the house and at the same time—again in my imagination—with nary a soul far and wide, to quote the poet Uhland, shouted in joy, in rage, mostly without words, simply shouting, the shouts exploding out of me. But as an avenger I now opened my mouth, rounding it, pursing it, stretching it, twisting it, tearing it open, silent all the while, performing a time-honored ritual, certainly not what I would have chosen on my own, a performance that during my time in front of the mirror had taken on an actual rhythm. And this rhythm had eventually generated sounds. From me, the avenger, singing had issued forth, a wordless singsong, a menacing one. And that was what had brought on the heartache. "Stop that singing!" I shouted at my image in the mirror. And it promptly obeyed, breaking off its humming, though that made my heart twice as heavy. Now there was no going back. "Finally!" (Another shout.)

The moment had come to sally forth to seek revenge, the campaign to be carried out by me and me alone. For the first time in a decade, instead of just showering, I took a morning bath, then donned, one leg and one arm at a time, the grayish-black Dior suit I'd laid out neatly on my bed with the white shirt I'd just ironed; on the lower right side the shirt had a butterfly embroidered in black, which I pulled into sight just above my belt. I shouldered my carryall, which itself weighed more than its contents, and left the house without locking up, my practice even when I expected to be gone for a while.

Yet I'd come back only three days earlier, after spending several weeks roaming the northern interior of the country, to my chosen home on the southwestern outskirts of Paris. And for the first time I'd felt the tug of home, I, who since the premature end, if not sudden termination, of my childhood, had been leery of homecomings—not to mention one to my birthplace—indeed had had a horror of any kind of homecoming—a clenching sensation in my body down to the last reaches of my intestinal tract—especially there.

And these two or three days after my belated but, for the first time in my life, not so much happy (get thee behind me, happiness!) as harmonious homecoming had reinforced my awareness of being where I belonged, and once and for all. Never again would anything disrupt my sense of being settled in and attached to that place. It was, quite simply, pleasure in the place, a stable pleasure, and that place-pleasure grew with the passing days (and nights), and, unlike in the nearly three previous decades, was no longer limited to the house and grounds, didn't depend on those at all, but pertained purely to the place. "How so? To the place in general? The place specifically?" — "The place."

What added to my unanticipated place-pleasure, not to say faith in the place (or, if you will, my late-blooming local patriotism, of a sort more likely to be manifested by certain children), was the fact that in this area yet another of the new holidays that had been proliferating in recent years, and not only in France, had just been announced, tacked on not to the long summer holidays but to those around Easter, themselves already not that short, and now extended, in this year of my tale of revenge, to include the period leading up to the first of May.

With many people away, the place felt more spacious, expanding from day to day, and at moments, standing for an entire day, losing its borders altogether. Days went by without the eruption of that two-dog barking on the other side of the hedge that would cause my hand, writing out words or numbers (on a check, a tax form), to jerk suddenly and scrawl a line—and such a thick one!—clear across the sheet of paper, whether a check or whatever. When a dog did bark, it was way off in the distance, reminding me of long-ago evenings out in the country, which now added to my awareness and space-sensation of homecoming, or of a homecoming in the offing.

In this period fewer people were out and about; far fewer. Sometimes from morning to night I'd meet only two or three on the street or on the usually crowded square in front of the station, and most of those were strangers. But didn't the occasional person I knew from sight also walk, stand, or sit (mostly sit) like a stranger? Like an entirely different person. And whether acquaintances or strangers: we never failed to greet each other, and what a greeting it was. Often people asked me for directions, and I could always oblige. Or almost always. But when I wasn't acquainted with a particular location, that very fact gave me and the other person a jolt of energy.

During three full days at home I didn't once hear the clattering of helicopters from the military air base on the Île-de-France plateau transporting state visitors to or from the Élysée Palace down in the Seine valley. Not once did the spring wind waft snatches of music from the airstrip to "us," as I involuntarily thought of my fellow residents and myself: the solemn music played as coffins containing the remains of soldiers killed in Africa, Afghanistan, or elsewhere were unloaded from state aircraft onto the platform of honor known as the "tarmac," to be welcomed home by the French fatherland. The sky, at mid-altitude, crisscrossed, darted across,

PETER HANDKE

flitted across (the first swallows), shot across (a very different kind of shooting and not the belated arrival of falcons and other taloned birds) by almost all imaginable birds, although—yet another absence—this time no eagle, otherwise circling summer after summer alone through the empty sky way high up, at the sight of which I'd once, at noon on a soundless day in high summer, thinking myself equally alone on the ground, had a vision, rather apocalyptic and certainly terrifying: it occurred to me that in the eye of that immense eagle I was the last human here on earth, spotted through the last remaining celestial opening.

And—to regain the local asphalt and cobblestones underfoot after scanning the heavens that way—in this entire period no crashing of garbage cans at the crack of dawn, none of the constant rumbling and roaring in the background, but rather, if any racket, only an intermittent one, now seven side streets away, now three stone's throws away past the second traffic circle, and now, after a dream or two between waking and sleeping, the garbage can by the door of my nearest neighbor, the one who in his entire adult life, actually quite long, hadn't once, so far as I knew, ventured beyond his house and this town: but here, and with the few others out there, neither a banging nor a clanging as they were emptied, as if there were hardly anything in them, just a brief whoosh, then a rustling, almost a chirping, not unlike a secret chiming; and finally the gentle sound of the cans being set back on the ground, probably also thanks to

12

certain local trash haulers who from time to time raised their glasses to me in the railway bar. And then the continuation of these dozy images, setting the mood for the day.

Time and again in my life I'd recalled the old more or less biblical story of the man whom God or some other higher power seized by a shock of his hair and whisked away from his accustomed place to somewhere else entirely—another land. And as for me, unlike the hero of that story, who I think would have preferred to stay put, I'd wished that I, too, could be spirited away, grabbed by a shock of my hair and transported by a merciful power through the air to live somewhere else? Not to live! Just to be swept away from the here and now!

During the three days before I set out to put my plans for revenge into action, I grabbed a bunch of my hair almost hourly, though not to lift myself off the ground and whirl myself away, over the horizons, but to anchor myself or keep myself grounded, standing on my own two legs in the here and now and, miracle or not, feel at home for a change. Every morning, as soon as I got up, I seized a shock of hair, first with my left hand, then with my right, pulled and shook it, hard and harder, perhaps looking to an observer like a person about to rip off his own scalp—yet it produced a well-being that gradually spread through my entire body, from my head down to my thighs, knees, and little toe, and not only the little one, fulfilling me, quietly pounding, soundlessly drumming through me with a sensation of being rooted in place, a sensation threatened anew with every passing hour.

To complement this oddity—a different one turned up every couple of years, opening my eyes to new possibilities—I noticed from one day to the next that among the houses orphaned during the two-week Easter holidays, one house appeared to be occupied. As if it were a local rule, or even a local law, whenever I'd passed a dozen lowered shutters and the like, I'd come upon a house where at least one window, if not all the windows, especially those on the ground floor, let me see inside, into living and dining rooms. Because the curtains were also drawn back, seemingly on purpose, the sight had something welcoming, indeed inviting, about it, whether tables were set or not: "Come on in, whoever you are!" Yet these rooms never had anyone in them. And this very absence of occupants tempted me to come closer and whetted my appetite—for all sorts of things. It seemed unthinkable that somewhere in the expanse of a house like that, the male or female owner or the couple, the entire clan, might be hiding, spying on me, whether in the flesh or on a screen. Although I always felt seen, the gaze was well-intentioned and accommodating. These houses were unoccupied only for the moment; in another minute I'd be welcomed from a completely unexpected direction, whether in French, German, or Arabic (any language but English). And the voices of children sounding as if coming from high in the treetops.

And once, on the second or third—and, for the present, final—morning of my return and homecoming, in front of just such an unoccupied hospitable house, in the tiny front yard, where the grass grew like grass instead of aspiring to be a lawn or such, a barbecue grill, looking as if recently improvised out of iron rods as in olden times, was smoking, two plumes of smoke from side-by-side fires, with one plume rising straight into the sky in classic fashion, the smoke even and bright, while the other plume was pressed toward the ground, likewise in classic fashion, dark and sooty, if only initially, as it left the fire: for after that, this second plume, swirling along the ground in twists and turns, in contrast to the antediluvian tale of fratricide, made its way into the sky as well, the blackish smoke, puffing hither and thither, giving way to white, bright, feathery cloudlets, (almost) indistinguishable from the halfway transparent plume from the other side of the grill, its twin, and, even more astonishing, a truly unprecedented phenomenon: higher up the two smoke plumes actually joined for a few moments and intertwined, over and over, in ever new configurations, just before they both became completely transparent and vanished into space, as the next smoke rocket and its companion rose from the grill below.

And lo and behold: the person who now came out

of that seemingly empty house and invited me into the yard for a treat was my former letter carrier, *la factrice*, followed, a few steps behind her as usual, by her husband, likewise *un facteur*, she having retired a few months ago, while he'd been pushed into retirement years earlier. I still have the note in which she, "*votre factrice* Agnès," informs us, the residents of the area, that she, who always covered her route by bicycle, would make her last rounds, *tournée*, "on 10 July 2020," and when I thought at one point that I'd lost that slip of paper, I, who've lost so many things in life without experiencing any regret, felt almost heartbroken—and how it cheered me when from amid the piles and piles of papers, without my hunting for it, that particular note surfaced and is now lying in front of me on my writing table. The three of us sat in the yard again until late afternoon, and the two former letter carriers described how they—he from the Ardennes in northwestern France, she from the mountainous region in the southwest—had been recruited by the national postal service to come to the outskirts of Paris and the Île-de-France, untrained country folk who, however, were hardier than residents of the metropolis and ideally suited for delivering the mail by bicycle—in those days unmotorized, obviously—pedaling up and down the innumerable inclines characteristic of the greater Paris area and known in bikers' terminology, including that of the Tour de France, as *faux plats*, false level stretches, the hills almost invisible to the eye but all the more noticeable on a bicycle.

Though summer was still some way off, I recall this one day, indeed all three days, as the longest of the year: as if each night were delayed past the natural divide between day and night; as if the sun, "seemingly miraculously," refused to set, at least until I was present for the next happening in the village, and then another, and another. And when night came on, there was no sense of its getting dark.

Again: lo and behold! The shutters were still lowered on the house next door, where the husband and wife who'd built it had died in quick succession ten years earlier—the excellent paint job hadn't begun to peel yet—but across the overgrown garden, where here and there a rose bush was coming into bloom, more splendid than before, a clothesline had been strung, crowded from one end to the other with children's clothing, most of it in dark colors, clothes that at one time would have been described as "shabby."

And listen: along the wood roads in the hills the creaking and squeaking of tree limbs as the wind rubbed them together, echoing the hospitable opening of garden, house, and wine-bar doors all through the area (the fire pit I'd seen earlier hadn't remained the only one).

And take a look: the clearing from which the clicking of hundreds of boules would usually have made itself heard was deserted except for a car parked on the edge, and behind the steering wheel a man sat motionless, his eyes fixed on the clearing, on the broad graveled surface grooved by the balls; he seemed to have chosen this spot

the way people from inland Portugal are said to drive
to the coast, their only plan being to sit in their cars for
a while without getting out, simply to gaze at the ocean.
But isn't the man in the car in fact Portuguese, a mason, who unlike today often has cement dust in his hair
when he sits of an evening on a stool near me in the bar
at the railway station?

So listen, will you: that rushing sound under the
side street: that can't be the sewer, can it? — But what
is it then? Where's the sound coming from? — It's coming from the brook or little stream that over millennia
carved out our rather small upland valley, flowing from
its source higher up, near where the palace now stands,
from Versailles down to where it empties into the Seine.
The brook was covered over more than a century ago.
— So it's our Marivel hidden underground that we hear
rushing that way? — Yes, that's the one, that's its name,
and see that curve in the street over there: it marks the
exact course and curve of the Marivel. What a rushing.
You won't hear a toilet being flushed, a washing machine
on the spin cycle, a fire hose rushing that way; only a
brook can make that sound. And in no time you'll see
its water, have it before you, out in the open, where you
can wash your face with it, drink it (no, that's probably
not such a good idea). — How so? — Look over there, see
that pump, the cast-iron one in the overgrown yard? Go
and pump it! — But it's all rusty. — Just brush off the
rust and keep pumping. — Now something's coming;

it's a muddy slurry, shit-brown. — Keep pumping, little pumper, keep pumping. — Well, will you look at that!

These unstructured days were coming to an end, however, and I sensed that most keenly when I looked from the street into the schoolhouse and saw the class-rooms, still empty at the moment, but not for long. The large windows had already been washed, the floors and desks mopped or wiped down. Yet this image of time about to run out, like all the other local images of transitoriness, had nothing depressing about it. Stacked in layers on the windowsills and elsewhere were books, at-lases, and other "instructional materials," not in new ar-rangements but rather in their time-honored places, and from a corner by the blackboard gleamed a globe; and all that, including the sparkling windows and the neatness of the bright classrooms as they waited quietly, commu-nicated itself to me, standing outside, radiated a joy in learning that had nothing to do with me personally, or if it did, with someone I'd been once upon a time, long, long ago — In reality, too? — Reality?

Lovely transitoriness, which at the same time, from one image of the place to the next, especially when the spot was deserted or closed off, awakened the impres-sion that here and there, and there, and there, a reopen-ing was about to occur, an undefinable one, but at any rate one that would let in a breath of fresh air.

It seemed like an eternity since the hotel and bar Des Voyageurs, diagonally across from the station, had been a real hotel and bar. The fourth and uppermost story had been converted into a rooming house, the residents glimpsed at most as blurry silhouettes. The handful of residents left on the lower floors were all the more visible, not as hotel guests but as stranded souls whom the government had billeted a good while ago in the rooms to the rear. At one time they'd constituted a slight majority in what in those days was still a hotel. But no new residents had joined them, and of the old residents whom the authorities allowed to stay on, beneficiaries more or less of the social safety net, most had died during the next two decades, the deaths usually taking place unnoticed in one former hotel room or another, behind windows whose glass had been replaced with cardboard or plywood; not once had I seen an undertaker (more than one would probably not have been needed) leaving through the side door (a feature only the Voyageurs still had). And the mourners at their funerals, if any, were limited to survivors from the neighboring nooks and crannies. It could happen, though rarely, that the deceased had relatives—a wife, a brother, a child—and they would be notified. But not one family member ever showed up at the cemetery. As seemed to be normal in such cases, we would hear that upon receiving the news, the former spouse, the son, even one mother, had silently raised their eyebrows or, on the telephone, likewise without a word, hung up.

Whether by mutual agreement or not, the cluster of three or four remaining residents, rather than hiding out in their rooms, could be found from morning to night and in almost any weather on the steps leading up to the glass door of the former Bar des Voyageurs, which was secured with chains and God knows what else. Until recently they'd actually formed a kind of cluster, the one on crutches hobbling from one step to the next, another constantly baring his one enormous tooth as he stared into the crowns of the plane trees, the third sitting, whether on purpose or because he couldn't help it, day in, day out under the very tree limb from which birds, the smallest as well as the largest, defecated until late at night: yes, the man was convinced he had to sit motionless on that particular step: it did him good to have bird droppings of various sizes land on his head, hands, knees, filled him with triumph to have sensed or guessed that a particular blessing was about to descend from on high and to have moved his forehead into position at just the right moment. And the four of them, or soon only three, were sufficient company for each other. Not one of them paid any heed to the rest of us as we passed on the station square. Every time I, who as time went by increasingly yearned for a greeting of some kind, tried saying hello to them as they huddled there on the bar's crumbling steps: no reply; "zero reaction." Fine: being ignored that way cradled me in security, preparing me for what was to come.

In the days following my homecoming, however: a transformation. It couldn't be ascribed, or not entirely, to the post-Easter blueing and greening. For during the

day it rained, poured, stormed, hailed (the hailstones
shattering the one intact windowpane in the old hotel),
and at night it turned bitterly cold. In the morning, as I
made my way to the bakery and the market stalls, dimin-
ished in number and with only slim pickings on offer
(see holidays), and passed the bar, I had a hallucination
or an illusion that the place was open. And the very next
moment I found myself sitting among the last of the
long-time residents on one of the steps, in a spot seemingly saved for me, neither at the bottom nor at the top.
They'd invited me to join them with incomprehensible
grunts—but no comprehension was needed—as well as
with sweeping gestures, yet I'd also joined them of my
own accord. A bottle of wine they were passing around
was proffered, not thrust under my nose but held out to
me, and without my habitual indecisiveness I accepted
it and drank. The wine, of which I took only one gulp,
probably tasted not that different from any wine drunk
first thing in the morning. But what's stayed with me
to this day is the aftertaste: the cigarette smoke I also
swallowed from the neck of the bottle. Not to be compared to the madeleine from the lost and regained time
of Monsieur Marcel Proust, yet a thing nonetheless, yes
indeed, a thing that would last, a thing I appreciated,
and still do. Wasn't there a song in which someone—
who can it have been?—sang, "life is very strange, and
there's no time"? — Wrong: "life is very short" is what
John Lennon sang. — But here I'm going to stick with
"strange."

I hung out for a while with the cluster or squad on the steps to the bar of the Hôtel des Voyageurs, closed as usual, and was shown hospitality, also as usual, without being expressly included in the circle by any one of the three—for a circle or group was what they formed. That day, in addition to me, someone else had joined them, a woman. I knew her; she came from the welfare agency, or whatever, responsible for the area, and presumably she was supposed to stop by the semi-ruin periodically to make sure things were all right, or whatever.

But this morning the woman seemed transformed. She didn't stand there, with her large, rectangular hand-bag over her arm, an official checking on those mandated to her care, but sat among them, her posture indistin-guishable from theirs, and she moved over matter-of-factly to make room for the new arrival. Like the others, she was smoking, at that moment reaching behind her without looking, as if she'd always done so, to help herself to a cigarette from the pack of the man sitting behind her. She looked completely at home among these weather-beaten figures (weather-beaten not only from spending so much time outdoors), at home as she hadn't been in ages, or maybe ever. In her life up to now, nothing had been the real thing. To be clear: this wasn't the real thing either, not yet. But it wasn't just a passing mood, whether brought on by the interruption in her routine due to the post-Easter holidays, which was opening up prospects as far as the most distant distances and vanishing points, or by who knows what else. Close to retirement in any case, she would leave the agency to its own devices, starting tomorrow—no, starting today! And what then? No thought of a then. Seize the day, no more rushing around! No need for company, or perhaps only for a gathering like this, which provided company, too, and what company! For she was experiencing the moment: "I will have experienced it," and how. And suddenly, as she turned her head toward the rest of us, sprawled around her, and gazed at each of us in turn, tears came to the eyes of the state employee she still was. She wept silently, without a sound, and if there was a sound, it was just one more of the small sounds in the circle, someone drawing on a cigarette, the glug-glug of someone drinking from the bottle—almost inaudible. She probably wept for only a moment, her eyes glittering behind her thick glasses, something not only I noticed: one of the other boozers on the steps of the former Bar des Voyageurs handed the lady an eyeglass-cleaning cloth, unfolding it with indescribable ceremony—a cloth that had clearly never been used, and was also, due to its larger size, far more practical than the cloths in circulation nowadays—and not until he'd let a suitable interval pass after the one or two tears had welled up (if that's what they'd been).

And once again I, the invited guest, sat there for a long time, passing the hours until the midday bells of the nearby town church chimed, which had been pre-ceded, toward ten in the morning, one of the usual times for funeral Masses, by the gentle clanging of the death knell, two single tones, one high, one low, repeated at measured, seemingly interminable intervals. Am I deluding myself in thinking that my fellow step-sitters didn't take in the bells? But apparently they didn't take in anything, not the rolling, then rattling of the commuter trains as they crossed onto the iron bridge just before the station—certainly not that, nor the repeated loudspeaker announcements in several languages, giving telephone numbers to call immediately if suspicious luggage or anything at all suspicious was noticed, which conveyed a sense of danger, of some threat, specified or unspecified.

I found myself remembering a narrative from the now long-gone nineteenth century in which the author imagines that whenever prisoners banished to an island in the easternmost reaches of the empire hear music in the distance, they listen to it with the certainty that they will never go home again. What brought that account to mind? Sitting here by the shuttered bar entrance with my hosts, who no longer took in any sounds but laughed louder and louder with each passing hour and finally in unison, in a raucous, clanking, groaning chorus, I imagined that the three of them, and eventually four (a woman's voice had joined theirs), were striking up this laughter out of their awareness that they would never go home. In this case being barred in perpetuity from going home (wherever that might be) gave them something to laugh about, something to warm the cockles of their hearts. These men were scoffing at the idea of homecoming, or any kind of return, in under- and overtones, at times mournfully, to be sure, from the heart, from the depths of the heart. Nothing could be done for them, in any way. And that was all right? They were salt of the earth of a special kind, useful for the here and now? And it was also fine, wasn't it, that they weren't decked out in costumes, whether red or green, or checkered, or in other colors?

All my life, whenever I was about to set out on what I considered a significant mission, I always looked first for what I also considered a necessary distraction, and always in nature. And so it was here and now.

From every open spot in our area, the eye traveled to the hills that formed a wide, almost complete ring around the upland valley. One of those hills, seen from the highest window in my house, stuck up above the others in the chain. But that appearance was deceiving; the hill just happened to be the closest. All the hills had the same elevation, and what's more they weren't hills at all, just creases projecting forward and back on the surface of the Île-de-France plateau, which surrounded the valley to the right and left: pseudohills; and similarly what looked like hilltops were illusory crests created by trees, more or less large and with more or less spreading branches that formed borders, or rather filigrees, against the sky. What looked to me from the aforementioned window like the highest hill was the illusion created, aside from the way the plateau protruded so prominently from the spot, reinforcing the impression of a peak, by a solitary giant oak, while in the distance distinctly smaller trees formed a horizon consisting of what seemed to be other hills: birches, maples, wild cherries, possibly looking even smaller because to either side of the oak on its promontory the plateau pulled back in an arc.

That this densely wooded line of hills, rising as if to the most distant horizons, and in almost all directions, was a mirage, and that its peak was no such thing: of this I eventually became aware, though only with the passage of years. Yet I continued to see and experience this ring of hills as it had initially appeared to me. The facts couldn't make a dent in the illusion. What I'd imagined proved durable, eventually taking on additional spatiality, materiality, color, and rhythm. Whether real or imagined: it worked. The highest of the hills, framed by the window, remained the highest, and the name that had originally occurred to me, spontaneously, almost as a joke, stuck over the decades, and by now had long since become an idée fixe in and with me: the Eternal Hill, the Eternal Hill of Vélizy.

In the three days after my homecoming I sat every morning, freshly showered, combed, and properly dressed, by that upper window. With both casements open wide—otherwise the bubbles in the old glass might have distorted the view—I took in the Eternal Hill without the crossbars in the way. It wasn't exactly contemplation I was engaged in, intentional or purposeful. So was it observation? Heaven forbid, certainly not that.

All too often, when I've progressed from merely looking and seeing to anything resembling observation, I've
felt I was engaged in something improper, even illicit, at
least for someone like me, and not only in my own eyes.
And besides, from the time I was very young, I've been
incapable of anything that might qualify as a scientific
gaze and, probably even more entirely, have lacked any
ambition in that direction. I've never had the slightest
desire to say, "I see something you can't see!" My desire,
if I have one at all: to become aware of something by
chance, yet, as described above, incorporate it fully into
my imagination, once and for all, and then, under the
spell of its image, drift off into a waking dream, awake to
a degree unmatched by any other kind of wakefulness.

In the days before I sallied forth to seek revenge, the
trees on the Eternal Hill had turned green—in a process rarely seen except in time-lapse photos, one lurch
forward at a time—and on my last morning the infinite
shades of green, varying from one species to the next, in
full sun and a westerly breeze and with not one house
to distract one's eye, extended skyward in waves to the
unwavering, pure blue. And not only did each green—
that of willows, alders, and poplars at the base of the
hill, of beeches and ashes halfway up the slope, of
birches, oaks, locusts, rowans, and Spanish chestnuts
everywhere—glow, shimmer, gleam, even gray! differently, but each kind's foliage—dense here, sparser over
there—also moved differently: swirling, fluttering, ris-

ing, falling, as if borne uphill by the waves and currents of the shadows that furrowed the fresh leafage.

"There it is!" I said to myself silently. "That's where it's going on. That's where it's happening." And already hesitation. "*What's* happening?" — "It." And at the same time, with my eyes closed and the hill promptly gone, I saw what I'd been missing, and not just in the last few days and even more the nights, missing sorely, as something lost and gone for good, and only to me? "How can that be: seeing something that's absent?" — "Yes! And not yet a thing but a term!" — "Could it be Eternal Recurrence?" — "No! What I saw, as a term and a thing, was the continuation." — "Eternal?" — "No, just the continuation. Onward to the continuation!"

I sat by the open window for a long time, a very long time, until late morning, without stirring. Every treetop on the hillside revealed itself to be a windmill. And the mills ground and ground. What were they doing—grinding out the continuation by any chance? Yes, indeed: the continuation. And just as a different shade of green predominated from tree to tree, each kind of foliage ground, swirled, circled, and gyrated in its own distinctive way. "Every bird flies differently?" Yes, and the leaves of those windmill trees likewise dipped and whipped, swayed and sashayed entirely differently from one to the next.

It was getting warmer, and in the middle ground between the open window and the Eternal Hill I saw, for the first time in the year, that tiny butterfly couple that I'd dubbed the "Balkan butterflies," because as they flitted up and down, seeming to become three, if not four, they reminded me of the Balkan shell game. In their pas de deux—or whatever it was—the couple came closer and closer to me, their increasingly tight and frenetic spirals escalating to a fury—or whatever it was—and finally, only a hand's breadth from my eyes, to such speed that the bright dots on their wings flashed like lightning, at which point, as in a flip-flop image, for the climactic moment of maximum speed, the circling seemed to come to a halt, motionless or beyond all motion. And I was filled with nameless delight in my current inactivity, and in the prospect of remaining inactive and letting things take their course, and on and on, et cetera and so forth.

For the rest of the day—can science possibly explain how and why that happened?—I was assailed by the images and names of towns, cities, and especially villages I'd encountered in the course of my life. Not one of the images represented a specific memory. There was nothing to remember about those places. I'd simply experienced them. Neither had I come to a realization there, even the most insignificant, nor had anything happened to me, not so much as a thwack on my ankles as a swinging door hit me from behind. It was more the place names that kept poking at me, and only in connection with the names did dim images appear, of the rises and dips in a road or a wagon track, of a plank without a railing laid across a brook, of a pockmarked dartboard in the corner of a bar. Yes, those place names, usually multisyllabic, transmitted more vivid images and contours than the nebulous visual auras or features associated with them. Circle City, Alaska; Mionica; Archea Nemea; Navalmoral de la Mata; Brazzano di Cormons; Pitlochry; Gornji Milanovac; Hudi Log (= Evil Place); Locmariaquer: I'd experienced nothing at all there, whether good or bad—no love, no fear, no danger, no thought, no realization, not to mention any connection or, God in Heaven or wherever, any vision. I'd just grazed those places, happened to pass through, and if I'd spent the night there, only because I didn't know what else to do (or on purpose after all, because the place appealed me in my cluelessness?).

And lo and behold! on this one day, the last before my unforeseen departure, the silent swarms of name-images from places all over the world that I'd driven, hiked, and stumbled through came to me as proofs of my existence, if not of grace. You and your kind have existed, and will continue to exist, at least for today and tomorrow. To have images and names come flying at me this way produced something like satisfaction, and that also held true for familiar German names—Fischamend, Rum bei Innsbruck, Gernsbach im Schwarzwald, Windisch-Minihof, Mürzzuschlag.

Even before day's end, the image-flurry was gone. As I'd done every evening that week, with sunset approaching (coming later now), after I'd managed to stay inactive, I made my way to the Bar of the Three Stations.

The owner, reprising our tried-and-true game, flipped open his new suit jacket, where the label, in suspect capital letters, read ARMANI, whereupon I, falling into my usual role, remarked, "Quality!" and he replied, "*Comme moi!* Like me!"

For an hour nothing out of the ordinary happened. Whether in front of or behind the bar, almost without exchanging a word, at most an exclamation now and then, we watched the nightly soccer match on television. Usually the set was tuned to matches between English or Spanish clubs, unless Marseille was playing, the club from the city where the owner had arrived from North Africa's Atlas region half a century ago as a fifteen-year-old—fatherless, illiterate, unskilled—and had soon, thanks in part, as he said, to spending so many nights outdoors at first, gained a foothold.

The weekend was around the corner, and the Bar of the Three Stations (the bus depot made it two, and the nearby regional station "a few arrow shots away" made it three) was filled with an after-work crowd, filled at least by comparison with the already quite empty and increasingly deserted square between the bar and "our" commuter station. The impression that the bar was full probably came from the fact that most of the guests were standing, if not at the counter then a few steps away, to be close to the television screen. The only guests one ever saw seated, on this evening as well, were a couple off in one corner, looking furtive, seemingly trying to avoid being visible through the window.

For the time being each of us stood or perched alone, disengaged from the person next to us, set off from the other, and not merely in dress, skin color, or other feature. Only here and there a group, an almost disconcerting exception, always small, consisting of two or at most three coworkers spending their Friday evening together, foreigners: from Poland, Portugal, or elsewhere. But at least one thing we all had in common: we would never, ever take a vacation—see the depopulated square in front of the station. We'd spend the couple of weeks we had off either back in the village where we'd grown up or right here, but we wouldn't go to a vacation destination if you paid us. Never ever? Who can say.

I knew almost everyone in the after-work crowd, and some of them not just by sight. In what had become his customary place stood the former owner of the café attached to the station, closed now, its iron shutters more rusty from year to year; among the guests he was the quietest yet also the most communicative and open-hearted one, and at the same time seemingly incognito, not who he appeared to be. When I passed his old café during the day, I'd sometimes knock on the shutters—a quick tattoo that reverberated, one syllable, then another, and finally one more—imagining that my greeting would somehow elicit a response from the audibly empty, cleared-out interior.

Though it didn't always happen, after-work conversations did spring up once the match ended, as they'd already done during halftime. Adam, the Portuguese mason, electrician, roofer, carpenter, HVAC technician, etc. had met a woman six days ago, for the first time in who knows how long, and he counted off the six on his fingers for me, over and over. And how Adam beamed as he told me the story, a beaming that didn't come merely from his freshly washed hair and clean-shaven cheeks. He'd already been to her place twice. He'd also invited her out to dinner once, but the money for his trip home, by bus, tram, and train, had come from her, eleven-ninety, more expensive than what she'd ordered at the restaurant. "And today she's already called me fourteen times! The first woman who doesn't want money from me, and she's Brazilian, too!"

The managing director, or whatever he was, of a firm on one of the highest floors of a financial-services skyscraper in La Défense, the business district, the top earner in his company—or so he implied—also, in contrast to us fools, the one "in the know," now revealed, unexpectedly and unbidden, that he was trying to escape from those exalted spheres. Except that "they" wouldn't let him go, "not yet." His "skills" were unique and highly specialized, and they were still needed. Yet he felt inferior to the others "up there," who were interested only in winning and killing, yes, "I'm not at their level! I want to be somewhere else. Where? I don't know. If only I knew. But one thing I do know, and I've always known it: I want to lead a chivalrous life, *une vie chevaleresque*, and the people over there beyond the hills won't allow it, they don't know what that is, haven't the faintest notion of *une vie chevaleresque*. To be liberated from all that—but how? To escape from the killers on the top floors and become a knight—but how?"

As was my habit, I kept shifting my attention from what was happening indoors to what was happening outside, as far off as possible, yet directing my gaze less skyward than earthward. The most distant thing in view was the playground to the west of the station square, which on that particular evening involved literally looking into the sunset. But for a good while after the sun had gone down, I could see two children swinging there, and like the butterflies that morning the two now and then appeared as three, that was how fast they were moving, as if competing with each other, and the paler and then darker the horizon became, the higher and more energetically they swung. The epithet "far-swinging children" came to mind, and then "Homer," but neither his war-wrought *Iliad* nor the wanderings of Odysseus—not even his long-delayed return to his family—but rather a third Homeric epic, one that was never composed and never will be. Or might it be after all—though perhaps not in verse? And look at that: first one of the far-swinging children way up high, then the other. And the more darkness closed in, the higher the children soared.

Night had long since come, and in the Bar of the Three Stations, now gradually emptying out, I found myself, as not seldom happened on weekends, next to Emmanuel, the auto-body painter, who from time to time sent to my phone a poem he'd written, usually as dawn was breaking, before he set out for his workplace in one of the new towns a dozen stops away on the rail line.

"Manu" was the one in the after-work bar who talked about himself, if not the most at least the most earnestly. Whether only to me, as this time, when it was just the two of us, I can't say. What I can say: I knew various things about him that weren't limited to whether, if he was wearing a shirt, it had to be one that didn't need ironing.

Today I learned how he'd come by the apparent burn or indelible ink mark on his forearm: it was a tattoo, his only one. And he'd applied it himself more than four decades earlier as an adolescent, using *une pâquerette* (from *Pâques*, Easter) as a template: a daisy. And why had he decided to tattoo himself? With childhood over, he'd found himself being ostracized by all his agemates, and he'd always been at odds with his family—his father, mother, and siblings. He thought the tattoo would serve as a visible sign of belonging: I'm one of you! — A sign to whom? The other boys? — They didn't even notice, and no wonder: even back then the daisy wasn't recognizable. The message "I'm one of you" was meant for me myself. — And did it do the trick? Did you see yourself as like the others from then on? — *Mais oui*, but of course!

After doing his military service overseas, in the jungles of Guyana, then coming back to this area, where he'd been born and bred, and throwing himself into his work, Emmanuel had hardly ever set foot beyond the borders of the département. It had been decades since he'd gone to Paris, just over the hills, let alone to the ocean. Married? Not even once. Children? *Néant*. Women? He revered them, and if he mentioned a woman, only in vague terms, and those only positive. Anyway, it seemed that no woman had "gone with him" in quite a while, for what he told me now about his most recent encounter sounded like something from a chaste love song: with childlike rapture he pointed to the spot on his cheek, freshly shaved for Friday evening, that "she" had brushed with a kiss, and this special moment had occurred several months ago.

Childlike, also boyish: that's the kind of person he was. And at the same time I pictured, and not only on the night in question, something I'd never pictured in connection with anyone else in our area: that this Emmanuel would one day, indeed soon, kill someone. (But wasn't there another person, too, a third murderer or killer? More about that later, perhaps . . .) And I had no explanation for this vision, certainly not the fact that in crime movies, at least the old ones, the murderer's pupils often disappeared under his lids, leaving only the whites showing, as was also the case with my friend.

I'd broached the subject once before, and he'd just laughed at me. But his first reaction to my tentative, somewhat playful allusion had been an almost imperceptible start, a sudden recoil. And now, next to him in the bar, at a distance from the others, also from the

owner—who never missed a word of any conversation—
I asked him, "Have you ever killed somebody?"

I had no idea where this question came from so suddenly, with a start of my own. I had nothing particular
in mind, not yet at least. But this time the question was
no joke. This was serious. "It's time to get down to business," said a voice inside me. "Adieu, sweet inactivity."

"Yes, I did once," he replied, "in Guyana, and not
on purpose, but I still feel terrible about it: a snake. It
was a present from a woman, on my last day there in
the military, a jungle snake, a tame, harmless, beautiful creature, with markings like bark. The woman had
put a cord around the neck of the snake in the crate, so
when I got back to France I could take it for walks. That
same night, in the dark, without intending to, I tugged
on the cord again and again, I don't know why, maybe
playfully, and the next morning I found my dear snake
strangled. I'll never get over the guilt!"

"And back home in Oran I murdered a swallow
once," the proprietor chimed in; he was sweeping the
floor at the far end of the counter. "I'm not really sure,
though. The swallow was perched with other swallows
on a power line quite far away, and I was standing at
my mother's window, aiming my toy slingshot at it, or
maybe just at the wire? And suddenly, without meaning to, I sent the pebble flying, and where one of the
swallows had been sitting was a gap! Good Lord, that
startled me, and of all the times my mother slapped

me, that was the only time I didn't even whimper." (*Both stories translated from the French.*)

As I continued to interrogate Emmanuel, I lowered my voice more and more, and not because I didn't want the owner, Djilali, the "exalted" or "mighty," to hear me. I spoke softly, but all the more distinctly, articulating every syllable: "Would you kill someone for me?" He didn't even shake his head, just laughed curtly, both at the suggestion and at me: if I was joking, it wasn't a good joke. And he turned away. I pressed on: "And if I pay you? Ten thousand? Fifteen?" In response, my friend the auto-body painter, looking at me over his shoulder: "What in the world can this person have done to you that you want him dead?" To which I replied, "The person didn't do it to me, or rather also to me, mainly to me, but that I'm used to, I even don't mind now and then, it does me good: but this person did something, and more than merely an injustice, to my sainted mother, my blessèd mother!"

Now I was really getting down to business, and more earnestly with every word, as I suddenly spoke out loud what I'd been keeping to myself for years (not necessarily thinking about it all the time, but certainly at regular intervals), and forged ahead: "The person who insulted my mother, and in words that stripped her of all honor, needs to be gotten rid of. It's time—if not tonight, then tomorrow, or at the latest the day after!"

The owner spoke up from a distance, where he was

drying glasses with a dish towel, his voice booming like a stadium announcer's: "*Matâ!* Kill! With a sword. *Mah al-saif.* Off with his head!" He didn't ask for details; in his eyes, insulting a mother deserved nothing less than death. Nor did Emmanuel interrogate me further, and although his own mother, and mothers in general, meant nothing to him, his expression, as he looked at me over his shoulder, suggested that he understood me, or at least my whim—except that it was no whim. And then he remarked, "That's something you have to do yourself," again making it sound like the playful exchange with which our dia- or trialogue had begun. "For a thing like that you can't just rent a killer." To which I responded, crying out this time: "No, it has to be a murderer for hire! As the son, I shouldn't have to carry out the sentence on that woman, and I don't want to!" At which the patron and the owner exclaimed almost in unison: "So it's a woman, is it!" After that no one said anything for a while. And suddenly a stranger who'd been eavesdropping offered to kill the woman who'd committed this capital offense, free of charge and for real. But taken aback I then lied, "It was just a joke!"

We stayed in the bar till almost midnight, and not only the three of us but also some late arrivals, for instance three garbage collectors who'd finally finished their routes, crisscrossing the upland valley, and now, who knows why, treated me and the others to a last—no, never say "last"—round. On television *Rio Grande*, with John Wayne, was playing with the sound off, which moved one guest to exclaim, "Look at that man's walk, will you!" whereupon the owner remarked, "*Comme moi*, like me!"

On the way home I made a point of passing through the station; the last train, to Saint-Quentin-en-Yvelines by way of Versailles and Saint-Cyr, hadn't come in yet. I went through the underpass and then checked out the platforms above, looking for the person I'd been picturing, along with Manu, in the scenarios playing out in my head, as the instrument of my revenge. But I was looking halfheartedly, because so much time had passed since I'd run into the person that I thought he was gone for good, probably dead. Earlier I'd usually been able to count on seeing him, after the last train, hiding somewhere in the semidarkness, behind a wall bump-out or a pillar, out of range of the security cameras. But every time he saw me, he would speak up, asking softly, as if my well-being mattered to him, how I was faring. One time, when he emerged from behind his pillar—in my company he felt he no longer aroused suspicion—I asked in return where he lived, and received the usual answer the homeless give: "*À gauche et à droite*, to the left and to the right." In both summer and winter he wore the same thin, quite clean garment, see windbreaker (an appropriate term in this context), and often shivered with cold, and not only in December, but his voice was always gentle and confiding, pet-like. He'd worked as a cook in many cafés, never in Paris proper but in all the suburbs, south-north, east-west, even in those days one week to the left and one to the right, though in a different sense. That had been long ago, and for ages he'd been living on who knows what, invisible during the day and emerging toward midnight from the shadow of a pillar or a wall niche in this station or the next. No kitchens were smaller than the ones in some of those cafés—even a ship's galley would feel spacious by comparison—and they were usually located on the lower level, near the toilets, and one time, when I caught him gazing at me again from one of his subterranean hide-outs in the station, his eyes very wide, I saw him, just his head, through the window in a café's kitchen door, with his toque on his black African head, and not facing the window but in profile: nothing else in the image but his head, bent over an invisible frying pan or some other utensil, the image blurry, distorted by the steam beading on the inside of the window, yet he was all the more obviously concentrating, like the born chef he was, on his task, which was now no longer his and never would be again, no matter how passionately he shared with me his various culinary tricks and techniques, his original recipes. Or, who knows, maybe he would cook again? He wasn't old, not by a long shot. Back to Africa? Didn't they need magicians there who practiced a different kind of juju, magicians like him? Stylites who huddled behind pillars instead of atop them?

During our last few midnight encounters Ousmane had frightened me—not for myself but for him? No, it was more a kind of unfocused fear, without a specific object. The way he'd been living now for a year and a day, by day and by night (or not living), wasn't sustainable, or would soon, and from one moment to the next—a horrific moment!—become unsustainable. Something bad would happen unless someone took him under his wing. And this someone was me, who for a long time had been his only contact. How did I know that? I just knew. And taking him under my wing meant I was supposed to give him a task. A task for money? He, Ousmane, had always rejected my (initial) offers of money, casually, not proudly but sternly: at most he'd sent me now and then to fetch him a midnight cup of coffee from the kebab stand, the only eatery near the station still open at that hour. And he wouldn't take money for the task either. The task was all he cared about. "I've been waiting so long for you to give me a task! You owe me that!" He didn't put it in words, just let me intuit it, not only from the look in his enormous, seemingly lashless, eyes but also from the roundabout questions he asked, more urgently each time and eventually in lieu of anything else, whether a greeting or any conversation: "Are you still all alone in your house? Do you have a big house? How many rooms does it have? How many burners on your stove? Is it on a public street or a private lane?" He wanted to be taken into my house, not as a vagrant, out of charity, but as a partner and business associate, and high time, too, after all our inconsequential, nocturnal palavers in the freezing-cold station! It wasn't that he wished he could live with me in my house; he demanded it. We would join forces, pull off something extraordinary. I should come up with an idea for him, and he, the chef, would make it happen, would make people sit up and take notice. The very last time we'd met, when he questioned me, seemingly as usual, about my house, Ousmane had barged into me from behind his pillar and boxed me, in the seemingly friendly African way, but so hard that I almost lost my balance. And for the first time I noticed this slender, emaciated person's outsized fists, and then his long fingers, accentuated by his almost white palms.

Had I forgotten that moment? At any rate, Ousmane mattered to me. He continued to be someone I valued, one of those people who in an instant, from being "he" or "she" could become "I," and "I" in turn could become "you! yes, my dear friend!" in an unexpected, unplanned reincarnation for that one moment I could spend an eternity describing. Ousmane's continued absence was worrisome. Yet at this particular midnight hour I was relieved not to find him behind his columns and pillars. He wasn't cut out for what I had in mind, which was nothing to be undertaken jointly; I couldn't assign it to anyone else. Yet it was a task, one I had to assign to myself.

To get home from the station I didn't use the sidewalk, choosing instead the double line that marked the median of the highway heading south, the road I sometimes called the *carretera*, sometimes the *magistrala*. The median strip, marked by day in dull white but phosphorescent by night, began past the underpass wide enough for a four-wheeled vehicle, gradually narrowing to a point on its way out of town, arrowlike, until near the turnoff to my house it had shrunk to the width usual for a median. I trotted along without paying attention to the few cars still on the road, which swerved to avoid me without honking or flashing their headlights, as if median joggers were a common occurrence.

Once in bed I fell asleep immediately. Dreamless sleep. All of a sudden I found myself awake, more poked than startled, abruptly yet gently. No sensation of time's having passed or of any interval. Yet the illuminated clock across the room showed that I'd slept for more than two hours. No matter how I woke up, during the day but also at night, I usually knew exactly what time it was, often down to the minute—even as a child I'd amazed my whole clan in the village—but this time my guess as to how much time had passed would have been wildly inaccurate, either far more or far less. Was the moonlight to blame? After all, I'd fallen asleep so fast that I'd neglected to close the blinds. But there was no moon, let alone a full moon. Or was it the hooting of owls, reverberating through the house from the Eternal Hill? No, not that either: owl calls as wake-up calls: impossible; the long, drawn-out sounds of those post-midnight birds had always deepened the silence and lulled me into the most peaceful sleep imaginable.

I lay there wide awake, the epitome of calm. Under ordinary circumstances, when a seemingly firm decision or unshakable certainty came to me during the first half of the night, waking up, whether in daylight or, far more often, in the second half of the night, would cast everything into doubt. And not that alone: what I'd thought through earlier, seen clearly, been sure of, decided upon irrevocably, would be revealed to me, when I was inevitably shocked out of my sleep by a blow administered by a gigantic fist, as utter nonsense, untethered from reality and presumptuous to boot, outrageous, the "mortal sin of pride." And that abrupt transformation occurring in the last hour of the night, by the gray light of dawn, was the norm, a law of nature as I saw it (which I'd lost track of during the night).

But these were no ordinary circumstances. Late night and early morning be damned: the previous evening's decision remained firm. Taking revenge for the insult inflicted on my mother was no pipe dream. Time to get a move on, and no rest till the deed was done! All those years of just toying with the idea, though in earnest, deadly earnest: that was over now. But hadn't the statute of limitations run out? — Nonsense: a crime like that was subject to no statute of limitations.

But I mustn't act precipitously, a usual failing of mine in word and deed. Though I was itching to get out of bed, I forced myself to lie there, with both window casements wide open. The whooshing on the expressways crossing the plateau beyond the woods sounded quieter than during the Easter week just past, with the newly unfurled foliage acting as a damper; it was almost a rustling in comparison to the roar of traffic in win-tertime. No wind, yet a current wafted in through the window as if the air itself were blowing on me.

In the early light I polished my oldest, trustiest shoes, in which, though they weren't hiking boots, I'd crossed the Spanish Pyrenees, then continued south through the Sierra de Guadarrama and finally the Sierra de Gredos. For my morning coffee I treated myself to beans I ground myself, beans from the Blue Mountains of Jamaica that weren't merely delicious but also, in my eyes, possessed of healing powers found in no other coffee in the world, and not only on this particular morning. Remarkable how in this hour before my departure tasting and smell-ing took precedence over the seeing and hearing, look-ing and listening that normally mattered more to me. The smell of the shoe polish, like that of the Blue Moun-tain coffee beans, pierced me through and through, while the morning sights and sounds, even the most de-lightful ones, today meant little or nothing; they existed, but they didn't count; an image of any kind, a sound of any kind made no difference. And remarkable how, ap-parently in exchange for my lost sense of time, I seemed to have gained a sense for weights: I found myself weigh-ing in my hand each of the few objects I packed to take along, passing it from one hand to the other and experi-encing a previously unknown pleasure in "just the right weight" for my purposes or, now, the "ideal" lightness. And finally I, who usually couldn't bring myself to eat so much as a bite from early in the day until late morning

or even early afternoon, actually felt hungry, and under
the linden out in the yard consumed an apple, with intense enjoyment, an Ontario, as well as a piece of toasted
pain festif from the local bakery, with each smack of my
lips (that was how tasty this breakfast was) throwing my
head back to gaze into the sky, as if I were enjoying the
food of the gods. I ate the apple as you sometimes eat
pears, core and all.

Not a day without reading a book, picking out and
deciphering the words. Which of the books I was reading just then should I pack for the expedition? Hesiod's
Works and Days? The Gospel according to Luke? *The Window Over the Way* by Georges Simenon (not one of his
detective novels—this was no time for crime or detective stories!—and certainly not on this particular day!)?
Not Hesiod: after celebrating the Golden Age and the
less delightful Silver Age, he bemoaned the fifth and
last, the Age of Iron, I believe, as the worst imaginable,
and that was how the poet viewed his own age, twenty-
five hundred years ago. No, *Works and Days* wouldn't be
coming along. Nor would Luke's glad tidings, including
the Resurrection and the Ascension, and the ultimate
promise of salvation to the worst sinners; "to day shalt
thou be with me in Paradise"—some other time, yes, the
day after tomorrow for all I cared, but today: no! And
Simenon would distract me in that masterful, sly way of
his from accomplishing my mission—though I had no
objection to certain distractions and in some situations
considered them essential—but that kind of distraction

for the day ahead: no, no! It was to be a day without reading, or only accidental reading, reading in passing, words chiseled into a wall-stone, for instance. Yet I already found myself missing the sound of pages being turned, especially the rustling of India paper, a music like no other. No book today, my love is far away.

In contrast to all previous departures from my house and grounds, and the town, this time I didn't keep an eye out for signs and portents of any kind (or wasn't it the case that in the past they'd veritably jumped out at me?). When my shoelace broke, it didn't mean that I'd do better to stay put or that acting precipitously would prove my undoing—it meant nothing, nothing at all. I calmly inserted a pair of new laces; the old ones had been hanging by a thread for a while. And the coal-black cat that crossed my path? Bring on another! And wasn't the travel bag slung over my shoulder reminiscent of the cloth bundle that Leo Nikolayevich Tolstoy took with him a hundred years ago when he left his Yasnaya Polyana estate to die in the small back room of the railway station in—what was the name?—what difference does it make? And up there in the sky, that plane following another so closely, would it shoot down the first one any minute now, and that would mean war? Once upon a time it might have.

Nothing could deter me from setting out. But neither did I need particular encouragement. Some other time I might have read all sorts of things into the robin's flying back and forth across the garden, swooping close to the ground, right in front of me, as I made my way to the gate. This time I saw its game of diving toward me, then speeding away into the bushes and back, as a bonus, also as assurance that I was part of everything going on in the rest of nature, confirming me and including me in the action.

But what was the puffy little bird with the brick-red bib acting out for me? It was performing the role of "revenge trainer." Yes, a role like that existed, or if not, at least it did for the duration of this scene, in my imagination. And my imagination wasn't the only source; this performance recalled, memorialized, and recapitulated another, very different one, in the Old Testament, when the prophet Elijah or someone is in the desert or somewhere, and after a long wait finally hears the voice of God, but not in the initial roar of the storm, in lightning cracking or thunder rumbling, but rather, if I'm not mistaken, in the long stillness that sets in after the storm, and the voice of God emerges from that stillness as the softest rustling or whispering (I wonder what the Hebrew word was), or, as I imagine it, chirping.

This scene in the Bible is generally thought to demonstrate and symbolize that God makes himself heard not through the forces of nature and in a voice of thunder but rather . . . (*dot dot dot*). In Holy Writ the story continues in the following convenient manner: the whispering of God from amid the silence, in a voice that couldn't possibly be any gentler, gives the prophet in the craggy desert an imperious and urgent command: Revenge! Avenge me! Avenge my people!

I experienced something similar upon setting out that morning when I served as the audience for Robin Redbreast's performance. All around ravens were squawking, crows were crowing, chickadees were sharpening knives, Asian parrots were screeching, blackbirds were piping, jays were grousing, doves were purring, yes, purring, magpies were scolding, chickadees were hissing, who-knows-whats were drumming, but not a peep out of the robin as it elegantly looped around me, close enough to touch, whirring about me, ahead of me: no sound but the almost inaudible swish of its wings. And eventually the bird settled on a bare acanthus branch in front of me, at eye level, and fixed its beady eyes in that puffy head on me, without a single sound's issuing from its beak. One sound, then an unbroken succession of sounds, short, identical, rhythmic, coming from its rocking on the branch, from its urgent nodding with its whole body, not just its head, a nodding with all its might, finally audible as a delicate rasping, conveying the stern command, "Do it! Do it!" And the performance continued for a good while longer until the redbreast took flight in a flash, silently swooping off to the ivy hedge, where it had been building a nest for the last three days, and in its beak, as I noticed only now, loosely linked coils of pencil shavings; the abandoned branch left bobbing in midair.

Over the years it had become second nature to me,

every time I set out, to glance over my shoulder at the garden gate and back at the house, glimpsed through the trees. Between glances I would take several steps backward, counting them: sometimes nine, sometimes thirteen, borrowing freely from the numbers supposedly sacred to the Mayas in the Yucatán. On this morning, however, I dispensed with looking back and walking backward. Full speed ahead! Taking unusually large strides, almost like a speaker emerging from the wings and making his way to the lectern.

At the moment I felt completely in control of myself in a way I'd felt only at the rarest of times. So was a rare time like that about to begin? We would see. (We? All of you, and me.) I also had the sensation that every fiber or cell or whatever of my body was taut, a sensation I experienced less and less these days, by comparison to my youth—taut, and vibrating with a presence of mind that also signified readiness. My spells of absentmindedness, on the other hand, which had come over me even in childhood, had grown more frequent with age, an "age-related" phenomenon, or so I'd thought until recently, assuming an acute form in the forgetfulness that seemed to get worse from day to day, in my inability to lay my hands on so-called use-objects and recall their what, how, and above all where—until I came up with the explanation, or excuse, if you will, that it had less to do with me and my advancing age than with the sameness, uniformity, mediocrity, and, perhaps easier to get a handle on—or not that easy to get a handle on—

pointlessness or uselessness of almost all use-objects nowadays, with the exception of a very few vintage items or classic implements; in short, it was the fault of all the stuff produced these days, and in conjunction with that the pointlessness of most actions, both domestic and public, and as a result, last and horribly least, the appalling tendency to lose track and lose sight once and for all of old and young alike.

Explanation? Excuse? Whatever. With my departure, now, at this very moment, from house and home: my old presence of mind revived, but in an entirely new form: on the one hand preparedness, "prepared for the worst," as if anticipating a possible catastrophe, perhaps even war, which would be the last (also prepared to intervene)—on the other hand presence of mind as becoming instantly aware, in a repeating loop, yes, simultaneous awareness, of what? of nothing, nothing at all—at peace—impossible to be more at peace (on earth)—the embodiment of peace, an alternative incarnation. "Uncontested peacefulness": that's how I experienced it at any rate, with peace assured in advance, and the struggle, or whatever challenge lay ahead, seemingly left behind somewhere: altogether a solemn peacefulness, and I, setting out in the freshness of morning, initially headed who knows where, as part of it. A passage from Moritz's novel *Anton Reiser* came to mind, about a warm but overcast morning, "the weather perfect for travel, the sky hovering so low over the earth, the objects round about so dark, as if one's attention ought to be fixed exclusively on the road."

But how to explain now, before I stepped from the lane onto the *carretera*, the terrified reaction of the young woman up ahead, mincing along in high heels on the sidewalk leading toward the station, when she caught sight of me, who pictured myself as so peaceably solemn, and cringed, uttering a scream that couldn't possibly have been more shrill?

True enough: even as a child I'd had fantasies of violence, and they weren't anything like imaginings, to say nothing of those involving my stepfather, in which, after the nights when he'd chased my mother around the house, hitting her again and again—I can still hear his laugh—in the morning I would fetch the ax from the woodshed, and, as he slept off his drunken stupor on the floor by their marriage bed, bash in his head. And in the last few years in this different country I, the foreigner, the stranger, upon hearing the often incessant barking and yapping of the local, unmistakably local, dogs in nearby yards, couldn't shake off the fantasy, which, by the way, gave me no pleasure, of striking the offending local house with a bazooka—though I must admit I haven't the faintest idea what a bazooka is or how it works—and blowing it sky-high; flattening it, turning it into a blazing inferno, accompanied by the howls of animal and human alike. And one of these days I actually will commit an act of violence (or not): smash the window of the yoga studio around the corner with one of the many chunks of curbstones left over from the days of the monarchy: as punishment for the shameless borrowing of lines from poems about trees—hubris—and spiritual equanimity, jumbled with Indian and Tibetan sayings intended to help one accept "all situations, all emotions, all actions, all beings," and interspersed with admonitions such as "Please arrive ten minutes early" and "Kindly remove your shoes before entering."

"I'm going to kill you (him, her)!" That curse I'd often had on the tip of my tongue in unguarded moments. But never had I voiced the thought, let alone spoken it out loud in the presence of others. If that ever happened, the curse would turn against me—of that I had little doubt—and I'd be forced sooner or later to commit murder or homicide for real. The recurrent dreams I'd once had about belonging to a family of murderers about to be found out—a multigenerational clan—had long since ceased, to my amazement, and almost regret.

I felt certain, who knows why, that I was born to be a murderer, whether the dreams had given rise to that certainty or resulted from it. But definitely not an avenger. Though a distinction should be made between avenging "myself" and "someone else." I can recall only one time when I avenged myself, and this memory can't be false because I remember nothing, absolutely nothing, about that revenge other than that it was a miserable failure, met with mockery by the one—no, by the girl—on whom I wanted to take revenge, and that happened with my very first gambit, my first ill-chosen word, which she summarily brushed aside, and me with it: a pathetic imitation, which couldn't have been more clumsy, of what a child (I) pictured as "revenge"; the child or garden variety of revenge.

Yet more than once, in later years, the impulse to take revenge for something that had been done to others. And those others, strange though it may seem, or perhaps not, were one and all members of the family, my mother's, or actually only her two brothers, drafted by the German half-the-world-spanning Reich and shipped off to Russia—"may the foreign soil rest lightly upon you!"—where they became cannon fodder, those brothers about whom she, their sister, told me story after story as I was growing up, speaking so lovingly that I, the listener, could almost see the two of them standing in the doorway. And she told stories and more stories. She told stories in the morning, she told stories in the evening, she told stories at night. And I was filled more and more intensely with the thought: revenge! But on whom? Whom could I attack, with those responsible all out of reach long since, if not from the very beginning? And yet: revenge! And again: but how? In what way? With what means, and how to obtain them? Whom to force to make amends, and how? And wasn't that a matter for the authorities? Leave the authorities and the bureaucracy out of it! But one kind of agency was certainly needed: the revenge agency, and that agency belonged to me. And again: ever more powerful motivation, and ever more powerful hesitation.

Never had I expected that someday this agency would be called upon to act in earnest. And when the

call came—that's how I experienced it—it happened under auspices completely opposite to those I'd pictured.
Something comparable (no, nothing's "comparable")
had happened to me once long ago, only once: I'd received an anonymous letter containing a threat to kill
my child if I didn't manage to bring back to life the six
million Jews murdered by my ancestors (that last part
only between the lines). I've written about that already,
but let it be repeated here, like various other things in
this story: because of the different place value. As I held
that letter in my hand, I guessed right away who'd sent
it, and set out with a jackknife in my trouser pocket or
somewhere, but that had nothing to do with revenge,
unlike on the morning in question. But why not? I
didn't know at the time, and I don't know today. What
I do know: there was nothing, and there is nothing, to
know. No why. Or: what took place was mechanical,
though not meaningless, and it gave way to relief when I
found myself standing face-to-face with the letter writer
in his open doorway, where he grinned at me without
a word while my fist clenching the knife in my pocket
relaxed into five, or five hundred, casually interlaced
fingers. No accusations, please, and above all no re-
proaches, and, for heaven's sake, no punishment. Punishment: that was never, ever for me. Taking revenge,
however—something altogether different—was burned
into me, probably by my mother's stories about her
brothers. But in this case, what needed to be avenged?

It didn't always stop at imagining violence. Now

and then I was also guilty of inflicting violence, just like that. Yes, violence had played a part in some of my actions, though far more frequently and ferociously in my words. And when words were involved, they were always spoken, never written, never the kind meant for publication, for an audience. To me, any writing of that kind, writing down, committing to writing, was always taboo.

Those acts of violence, the oral ones perhaps more powerfully than the brute-force ones, couldn't be undone by explanations of the sort that readily offer themselves and at times are even justified. Over the course of my life, what I more and more often saw as the epitome of violence, once actually suborning murder, was the language of newspapers, a public language deployed as if official and endowed with natural rights, far-ticking—shades of Homer again—without ever resorting to blatantly provocative formulations. The violence of this language, which presented itself as the only reliable one, all-knowing, all-interpreting, all-judging, completely objective, independent of works and days, slinging, looping, knotting, and tightening its signs and symbols, was what in my eyes was doing the greatest harm in the world, inflicting on its defenseless victims—what else could they be, given that kind of hands-off writing?—injustices from which they could never be made whole.

Yet a professional label like "hands-off writer" would have been quite to my liking, though coined for a hands-off writer of a different kind, a third or fourth kind. And what had brought to mind the imperative

"Kill!" was a passage in a newspaper article that was aimed at me but commented, in passing—in a subordinate clause, as I recall—that my mother had been one of the millions from the once "great Danube monarchy" for whom the swallowing-up of her country, now much smaller, by the "German Reich" had been an occasion for celebration; my mother, the article said, had rejoiced, which made her a supporter, a Party member. Nor was that casual aside all: the page on which this article appeared carried a photomontage with my seventeen-year-old mother's head enlarged and superimposed on an enormous crowd shouting Heil, or whatever, on Vienna's Heldenplatz, or wherever.

"You're right to see this now as deadly serious," I told myself in one of my silent conversations with myself as I paused where the lane met the highway: "But just as there's a time to love and a time to hate, isn't there, my friend, also a time to be serious and a time to play?" To this I replied, "Wrong, old boy. That I'm taking this seriously now, unexpectedly, I grant you, suddenly even, isn't deadly but rather bound to evolve into a special game, a game of games, which couldn't be played without this seriousness, never ever in life, a dangerous game, I grant you that, an incendiary game. But that's what the story calls for." — "History?" — "You fool!" — "Idiot yourself!" Whereupon a bird in one of the trees along the highway squawked the same insult, belting out, over and over, "Idiot! Idiot!"

All this time I'd managed to keep an eye on my ailing

neighbor's front door; it hadn't been opened in ages, but this morning the slippers that had sat on the doorstep in the same position for months were propped upright, leaning against the door; and across the street I could see the actual idiot, my counterpart, you might say, shifting a valise and a suitcase, the kind without wheels, from one hand to the other, as if he didn't know what to do with them; as if, his idiotic smile suggested, he didn't know what to do with himself either or understand where he'd ended up. I waved to him, and a gurgling noise seemed to be his response: "Bonjour!" And farther along, on the *magistrale*, another lone figure, an ancient man, standing there "for hours, since the first morning train" in the middle of the sidewalk, "like something ordered and not picked up."

Strange, or not strange after all, that when I first set out on my revenge expedition everyone I encountered was alone. (There was one couple among them, belonging to the category I'd labeled "modern couples": a dwarflike old lady—another ancient—feeling her way along, one step at a time, with her cane, her arm hooked in that of her companion, who was definitely youthful, at least by comparison, in high heels and with her hair blowing in the wind, which couldn't be said of the old lady's.) The buses passing on the *carretera* never carried more than a single passenger, and when I glanced back at the trains on the railroad embankment, in one compartment after the other I saw only single silhouettes, far off and farther still. So had I forgotten, as I drifted into the spirit of "Do it! Do it!", that today was the last day of the post-Easter or May holidays, and that not until the following day, which was Sunday, would all the vacationers be heading home?

But how did it happen that the animals I met, which usually turned up in multiples, also appeared only as singletons—with no others of their species far and wide? Look at that: the familiar Balkan butterfly, which otherwise could be counted on to form part of a couple swirling through the air and multiplying before my eyes, now fluttered back and forth alone, worrisomely close to the ground, the tar and the asphalt. What was going on? Enough questions. Don't ask, including when the iron garden gate clanged shut, a clanging that resounded and echoed through the entire area and beyond, taken up by the street wind I felt blowing in my face.

Worth reporting, or, more importantly, worth evoking, in one way or another, the solitary players from place to place, from playing field to playing field, from terrain to terrain. In the case of a basketball player, alone on the court, shooting from the left, then from the right, then from a far corner, then leaping from directly under the basket as he tried to dunk the ball: that was still a familiar sight, as was, more or less, the soccer player, alone on the pitch, time and again kicking, pushing, lobbing, playing the "leather" (if it was that) from the penalty mark into the unguarded goal. More striking was the man holding a tennis racket with no ball or net in sight—was he even on a tennis court, and if it was that, one no longer in use, long since transformed into an overgrown *terrain vague*?—repeatedly swinging his racket at invisible balls, and not in one direction but every which way. And what about the boules player, alone on the sandy court, ceaselessly tossing, hurling, and rolling his six balls, with one ball always knocking another or even all five out of the way, scattering them, a constant clicking in the silence by the edge of the woods, the sound also audible across many streets, squares, railroad tracks, and even on the far side of the expressway—or had it become a sort of "echo image" there? What these solitary players had in common was their similarity to marionettes. They stood there stiff-legged, or moved with raised shoulders, as if being pulled on strings, their arms whipping up and down, their eyes expressionless, unblinking, as they neither looked up nor cocked their ears.

By that time I was already somewhere else, long, long gone and far from my usual stomping grounds. At least that's how it felt. Yet hardly enough time to mention had passed since I'd left my house and the highway behind. "Give me a number!" — "Let's say twenty minutes," or thus: "in no time" I found myself beyond my daily haunts and confines, in an area that wasn't off-limits but also, at first sight, not exactly reassuring: alien territory, a foreign setting, yet one that — "There you go again, saying 'yet'" — was merely the next valley over, barely separated from my valley by a narrow strip of plateau, and like mine part of the Île-de-France, with the same high Île-de-France sky overhead, the same winds, primarily from the west, the same soils, the same trees, the same natural colors, the same house types, some charming, some hideous: Île-de-France, a country unto itself, a land island surrounding Paris (to be avoided on this day), whose shores I'd circled over and over and come to know intimately. "But now a 'zone'? A menacing one? Perhaps forbidden the moment I entered it?" — "Worse still: for a moment, which subsequently recurred for moments at a time: a death zone." — "How so: A person who sets out, bent on revenge, feels he's in a death zone?" — "Yes, in the death zone, he himself and he alone. That's how it was. And that's how it is." Venturing all my life into forbidden territory. And now: in the Valley of Death. Unlawfully. Illegally. And how right it felt!—right as never before. For secretly I'd always seen what I was doing as illicit, not outwardly, but deep within me, in the deepest recesses of my being. From the outset what I was doing was illicit; I was a born outlaw. And now, as I expressly and intentionally, of my own free will, crossed the border of illegality into the realm of crime, before the eyes of the world, or some other eyes, what I was doing would come to light, to blazing, blinding light, at long last. Way back in childhood a certain kind of crime had attracted me, filled me with enthusiasm, and this would be, and would also represent, that type of crime. Triumph! — "Were you maybe also drawn to the crime you were about to avenge, or what appeared in your eyes to be a crime, and in yours alone, a son's eyes?" — "No answer. Or maybe later. In a different place. In a different land." One way or the other: at long last I would give the hereditary or congenital outlaw in me free rein! Put that aspect of my nature to the test. Turn thought into action. Exercise it! Execute it!

A border crossing of this sort occurred when all of a sudden I felt in a hurry, for a change, to get out of my familiar area. Unlike countless times in the past, when I'd chosen to cross the plateau on foot, then hike down into the valley of the Bièvre and follow the river upstream toward its source, on this occasion I took the tram—the new line had been inaugurated barely a week earlier— from the station located three stories below the neighboring railway station in Viroflay. I didn't even bother with the stairs but let myself be transported into the depths by the spanking new escalator.

In the station below, the railbed had a single rail for each direction, and at each end of the platform the rails entered a tunnel as they left the station. When you looked up from the platform, your eye traveled up the stairs and the escalators, past the elevator shafts, and all the way to the roof, located approximately at street level; it was like looking into a dome, brightly but softly lit. The entire space, viewed from this minelike depth and as part of Greater Versailles, looked new, and not only the network of stairs and elevators, but also new in the sense of something that had never existed anywhere else, in this form or with this appearance, and certainly not as the place where you'd expect to board a tram. (That was my thought, and not only upon entering it for the first time.) Initially the place was reminiscent of a cathedral, far underground, and thus also of a catacomb. But these spaces, extending from below to above and seemingly (no, not "seemingly") multiplying from there, resisted comparison with any others; quashed, in their gentle way, any kind of comparison.

A tram station like this had never been built anywhere, or if it had—in Seoul or Ulan Bator or wherever— "No!" (I put my foot down.) The station's walls had been left for the most part unclad, none of the ceramic tiles omnipresent in the Métro or slabs of marble (or if there were any, I didn't see them). The earthen walls had been stabilized, then sealed to prevent water from seeping through, but otherwise left as if they'd just been freshly excavated—the digging had taken several years. And they weren't even perfectly sealed, those walls: here and there tiny trickles emerged from the composite of sand, rock, gravel, and concrete; and mosslike plants, clumps of grass, twigs (without branches or trunks), even algae, let's say, were growing out of the grotto-deep station walls, in glowing colors like those of plants in an aquarium, also undulating like them, at least when the trams pulled into and out of the station. Porous yet robust, more resistant, or resistant in a different way, to the ravages of time than concrete, "playfully resistant": that was how they presented themselves, these earth-sand-gravel-pebble-ledge walls deep underground in the side

valley sloping down to the Seine, promising a durability
rarely found in new construction, thanks especially to
their most prominent material, the same as that used in
the construction of many houses, nearby and through-
out the Île-de-France, that had been occupied for far
longer than a century and were still occupied by mul-
tiple generations, both native and foreign: sandstone in
shades of red, gray, and yellow, which at first sight looks
as though it's crumbling away (any minute now it will
break off the façade, taking the whole façade with it),
but is almost as hard as flint, with the seemingly crumbling parts actually weatherproof, knife-sharp edges.
And furthermore, these subterranean walls, bathed in
electric light, displaying surface textures and a play of
colors more heartwarming than daylight or even sunlight shining on the house fronts, outdone perhaps only
by the play of colors on the horizon in morning and
evening: the play of colors characteristic of sandstone,
incomparable combinations of yellow, gray, and red in
countless variations.

"Don't succumb to admiration!" Over the years that
had become one of my watchwords, almost a credo, and
applicable to more than just technical details. (Feeling reverence or "letting oneself be stirred or deeply
moved": that was something else again.) On the other
hand, I couldn't help admiring the *techne* of this tram
station, and also the technical details of how travel from
there worked, in the spirit of a sentence in an old movie
I recalled seeing as an adolescent, the words spoken by a

girl to a young man—weren't they Ophelia and Hamlet?:
"I can't help loving you."

With a sonorous humming, a sound so different
from that of trains and buses, as well as of the Paris
Métro, the underground tram glided into the station
from the tunnel. Contrary to my expectation, upon
boarding I didn't find myself alone in the car, another
respect in which it differed from the suburban railroad,
where sometimes, especially when I got on shortly before midnight, I'd step into a completely empty car and
literally breathe a sigh of relief, exclaiming silently, "Not
a soul! Terrific!" But on this morning I was cheered by
the prospect of starting my journey out of the area in
the company of others. Anything not to be playing sol-
itaire just now.

The tram's two cars were almost full, probably because the line and this stretch of it had gone into
operation so recently. Most of the passengers were
curiosity- or pleasure-seekers. None were on their way
to work or, like me, on a mission.

The trip through the tunnel took unusually long,
and not merely for a tram, so much so that I began
to wonder whether something was amiss, as I usually
did when a train lingered longer than it was supposed
to in a station, except that this time the situation was
reversed. My fellow passengers, however, acted uncon-
cerned, so I did the same.

I could feel, as well as hear, from the occasional
squealing of the wheels on the single track, that we

were going almost steeply uphill in the tunnel, and at the same time in curves, though gentle ones; the low-pitched purring remained the underlying tone, however. Finally we left the tunnel and emerged into daylight, and at that very moment the purring changed to a buzzing, even softer and equally harmonious, a musical, also hospitable, harping.

So the subterranean train had become a streetcar now? Not yet, not quite yet: yes, there were streets, two of them. But instead of running parallel and close to the tracks, they were far off, on slopes to the right and the left, hugging the edge of wooded areas, while the tram below traversed a wide depression, with hip-high grasses and bushes more than man-high on either side. Before the rail line was built, this stretch had been a regular, or rather a highly irregular, wilderness, an overgrown gully into which little light penetrated, and the approximate location of the railbed had been a rivulet prone to drying up completely during a drought.

In the past I'd often fought my way through this gully wilderness, enjoying the pleasure and sense of adventure that resulted not only from picking rowan-berries, chokecherries, and wild currants, all offering a special delight to the palate. One time, in the deep gloom, in a spot where the rivulet formed a vernal pool, a snake came toward me, dark black, long and slender, not crawling or slithering but bolt upright from its head to the midpoint of its body, gliding along amazingly fast through that seemingly trackless waste and still upright when I caught a last glimpse of it as it moved off elegantly and disappeared into marsh leaves as large as roof tiles. No tongue-flicking to be seen, but also no crown on the snake's gleaming black head, or maybe there was one: I pictured this creature as the local majesty swerving through the wilderness that had become its domain. Many a time after that I'd returned to the place where I'd encountered this phenomenon, hoping to catch sight of it again, but always in vain. Instead I conceived the conviction (not what you'd call scientific) that in the spot where a snake has been spotted this way it won't ever allow itself to be seen again.

When the tram project began, I was indignant at the way the gully wilderness was being cleared, leveled, and stripped of its natural contours. Since then, however, I'd grown fond of the new configuration, just as I came to like the subterranean tram station: the light carpets of grass, still treeless, spreading up and down the adjacent slopes, the drainage channel with cattails and more or less wild sword lilies along its banks, the gravel hiking path linking one of the streets to the one opposite, cutting straight across the former gully at a spot where the tram was still beneath the surface. If anything made me feel bad, it was a momentary pang for Her Majesty the slim, erect black snake in the dappled shade, and perhaps another pang for the wild currants. But the way the landscape had been altered: also beautiful; beautiful in its own way.

Now, as the tram glided along the hollow, I looked

out the window and saw three deer, hardly hidden among the savanna grasses and stalks; they were grazing calmly, in my eyes constituting a family, not one original to the place but one that had made its way there from a residual wilderness who knows where, seeking out the tram cut as if it offered greater safety. And forgetting everything else for the moment, I had the sensation I was on my way to a festive dinner, a new or rather new kind of dinner, and not I alone but all of us on the tram.

In my youth I'd focused an inquiring gaze on the space between streetcar tracks somewhere or other, and among the withered leaves and especially the grains of sand at my feet I'd glimpsed—strange, or not strange after all—an ocean shore and beyond it a distant horizon summoning me to an unspecified freedom and future, and now I thought I heard that same sand crunching beneath the tram car—even though, when we reached the last stop more than an hour later and I got off and bent over the rail, nothing but virginal steel gleamed up at me, immaculate, unsullied by a single one of those sand atoms or so much as a bit of down from a bird's plumage.

Not until it had climbed to the plateau and then begun passing apartment complexes, followed by more and more office buildings, did the tram, after its trip through the tunnel and then an almost equally long stretch across the open savanna, become an actual streetcar. And the loudspeaker announcements in all the cars contributed to that transformation. A woman's voice, on tape or from who knows where, intoned the stations' names, the timbre so unaffected, solicitous, and veritably warmhearted that I felt I was being addressed personally. — "By the woman or the station?" — "Both." And suddenly I recognized the voice. The woman to whom it belonged had once—long ago—been one of the not negligible number of female enemies I'd had in the course of my life. (Not from the very beginning.) Back then she'd been an actor, her only parts supporting roles. (Did such things even exist? And somehow or other she'd been satisfied with them, found her brief appearances onstage energizing, and sometimes spoke of them with unmistakable pride.)

Then, from one day to the next, she hated me. But she didn't leave it at that. Instead of pushing me away and hating me from a distance—she knew me and realized I'd feel her hatred no matter where she was—she came even closer, refused to let me be, and eventually began to stalk me. Soon the persecution progressed beyond heart-stopping phone calls in the wee hours of the night and the like. Whenever I went to open the garden gate in the morning, I had to steel myself for seeing her standing there, not about to ring the bell (which had been on the fritz for ages), but a few paces away, in the shadows cast by the spruces that lined the lane, staring at me out of black-rimmed eyes as if she'd been waiting for me for some time, and with one leg in front of the other, as if she were ready to get a flying start, except that the one time she hurtled toward me on her "pencil heels"—not an appropriate term—one heel got stuck in the gravelly sand outside the gate, and she tumbled headfirst (or was this an earlier woman or a later one in the series of those who became enemies, or mortal enemies—the one who, when we first met, read a rosy future from my hand, a future the two of us would spend together? or maybe the one who even before we were introduced had caught but a glimpse of me across a crowded, dimly lit hall, and, as she told me later, had immediately been overcome by a disturbing, almost uncanny uneasiness? or the one who, when after a long night I eventually found myself lying next to her after all, had merely remarked, "Well, what took you so long!?").

Each time one of those women conceived a burning hatred for me, I hadn't seen it coming, and each time I accepted it as a natural occurrence, though one I couldn't explain or figure out, and never really wanted to anyway. At most I initially toyed with explanations, for instance invoking the sentence from a story by Anton Chekhov: "She hated me because I was a landscape painter," or I fooled myself into thinking that somehow or other I seemed to hold out some promise, though my looks certainly had nothing to do with it, "something I can't possibly deliver, and no one can deliver." After that, no interpretations or explanations; even toying with any such thing no longer made sense. These particular women, these, yes, unique creatures—I continued to see them as creatures even more vividly than before—

had become my sworn enemies, without swearing, to be sure, but all the more fervently; they hated and persecuted me, and the hatred and persecution would never end until death did us part, and I not only understood that but conceded that they were right.

In the world of facts, however, with its days and days, nights and nights, months and months, that was no kind of life. The woman, never mind which, did her utmost to hinder me. To hinder me in what? In all my doings, in my daily undertakings as well as my quiet evenings, in the setting of the sun as well as the rising of the moon. In olden times people had a nickname for Satan: the Hinderer. The woman always turned out to be the hinderer, the one whose mission in life consisted of hindering. Destroy? Devour? Hinder, hinder, and hinder again: that was it. And if, in recounting my fantasies of violence, I've refrained from describing the specific fantasy prompted by each of these women, it's because no other situations brought my homicidal impulse so close to the surface, just for a second, but how!—so close to "Now! Now I'm going to do it!"

And again, I can't explain why each experience of being hemmed in and hindered by one of these hate-women, and the inaudible and invisible nature of it, didn't end as it had begun, "at one blow," but did cease just as suddenly. One morning, for instance, when before opening the garden gate I bent down and peered through the keyhole, as I'd been doing for months, to see whether the one-woman army was at her post, so I

PETER HANDKE

could gird myself for the full sight, it was over. All clear. Over and done with. And there was no explanation, not so much as a playful one, not even in the involuntary exclamation that burst out of me every time: "That's what's meant to happen." That's how it was. Not "worth mentioning" anymore.

From that moment on, my female nemesis would be gone for good. Not one of these enemies did I ever see again, including those who lived nearby, and, for all I knew, were still alive and still living there, one of them even in my immediate neighborhood. Mystery upon mystery. It's been a while now since a woman with whom I've formed a relationship has turned into an enemy overnight. And sometimes I catch myself, in the crowded Métro, in the local supermarket, possibly upon entering a waiting room, on the lookout for female devils from times past, bracing myself for the sight of one of them seated in the waiting room, leafing through an old issue of *Paris Match* and staring up at me "from below" like the sirens in Homer.

On the tram ride across the Île-de-France plateau, I now heard after all, for the first time in almost decades, the voice of one of them. How she purred, as at the beginning of our acquaintance, purred in harmony with the purring of the streetcar, muffled thanks to some technological innovation. Purr on, purrer, purr on. Play on, gentle harp, play on.

II

THE SECOND SWORD

The woman's accusations, lobbed past me on the newspaper page at my mother, had been a different story. I'd
never met this person, and that remained the case after
what I called "the crime." Today, however: yes, face-to-
face! Though her article had been accompanied by an
author's photograph, I had no mental image of her. Perhaps it was also because I associated her with the swarm
of militant feminists—picture the details for yourself—
that I had no face in mind, even before reading her
piece; and after I'd read it—actually more a question of
skimming, in the course of which the entire page leaped
out at me—the situation was no different; a jolt of rec-
ognition both undefined and indefinable occurred only
after I took off my glasses and the features in the author's portrait went blurry.

On this day, too, she wouldn't acquire a face, not
even in the moment when I'd be standing before her,
eye to eye but at a carefully calculated distance, which

I worked out in uneven numbers of paces: nine, seven, five, three . . . —now!

Her address, on the other hand, I'd had for a long time. Years after her atrocity I'd received a letter from her. Almost impossible to say what it was about, and certainly impossible to summarize the contents, if any. Not a word, at any rate, about her attack on me—which in any case meant next to nothing to me, let alone affected me—and above all nothing about the assault she'd perpetrated so casually, as if in passing, on the memory of my blessèd mother (yes, for the second time I use that word, and can't use it too often). In the attempt, now during the tram ride, to recall that letter, which I'd perhaps been expecting, if in a very different form, it seemed ("it appeared") that its purpose was to invite me, in polite, noncommittal terms, to a friendly public debate, conducted remotely, in writing, and that she "privately" (or did she use a different word?) now and then (her words?) also "sympathized" with me (the actual word). The only unexpected feature of the woman's letter was that she hadn't produced it with a computer or printed it in some other fashion but had written it by hand, in her own handwriting, as a hand writer. And precisely this handwritten character was chiefly responsible for the fact that there was almost nothing in the letter, as little today as when it had originally reached me: for most of the wording or words, especially those toward the ends of sentences, remained illegible. That wasn't the only thing, obviously (or maybe not), that made it impossible for me to write back. But it counted. And what didn't count at all: that you couldn't tell whether it was "a woman's handwriting or a man's." Hardly ever had I laid eyes on such a jumble of letters, a tiny illegible one after an equally illegible giant one staggering in the opposite direction, and vice versa: not in the writing of the sloppiest children or the shakiest oldsters, and certainly not in that of the dying; maybe there was one exception: the writing attempts of people born blind, but even theirs bore no resemblance to this mess.

Now I was on the way, or on one of several possible ways, to her, the one whose name and address were printed, "in boldface" or "light," on the yellowing envelope in my breast pocket: this woman and I had been living, and for decades, in the same region, the Île-de-France, she merely in a different part, the section called La Grande Couronne, or Outer Ring. Upon leaving my house, and even more as I walked to the tram station, I'd still felt as if I were being watched, and by her, the evildoer; but now, in the interval during which I was traveling to where she lived, with the thing in mind I had in mind, no longer.

That also had to do with the fact that as we progressed from stop to stop, I'd become one of many passengers on the tram, knew I belonged to this community, was one of them, one of us, as we crossed the plateau together, zigging and zagging, taking curves and forging full speed ahead, locals. At the same time

I was picturing Tolstoy, no longer the tottering oldster I'd pictured earlier setting out on foot for his last foray, with eyes that had already bid the world adieu, but the one wearing an eyeshade, strong and indomitable, and I wished, without hope of having the wish fulfilled—and a good thing, too!—for just such an eyeshade.

For this hour and beyond, I didn't need that Tolstoyan eyeshade, not yet. But what was the story with the woman sitting across from me, who suddenly jumped up and moved to a different seat?—Yes, she was annoyed with me, not because I'd been staring at her but because, on the contrary, during the whole trip I'd ignored her presence; not till she flounced away did I register her; and as I then observed, her jumping up and moving to another seat continued; I wasn't the only passenger blind to her charms.

With all the other plateau-crossing tram passengers, whether getting off or remaining seated like me, I felt I was in good company, however. Incidentally, it was strange, or not so strange, that from the station at the beginning of the line to the one at the end I had almost the same faces around me. Or did I merely imagine that? (No more questions, or at least not this kind.) And one and all we were quietly preoccupied, and not a few were just putting on an act, or they were actually not aware of what they were doing. The man engrossed in the book on his knees, not glancing up once, was holding it upside down, yet he moved his lips as if he were reading. The person over there whispering into his mobile telephone apparently didn't realize that his device, bandaged from top to bottom with tape, wasn't working, probably having gone to pieces ages ago. All well and good. Let him be.

Most of the passengers in our car were moving their lips more or less silently in their own ways, each with a different meaning. The thick-lipped man from Africa, pausing from time to time and raising his head to look out the window, then moving his upper and lower lip but without bringing them together, or if they did touch each other, ever so gently; he seemed never to ask questions and never to expect an answer, oblivious to the term or the concept "answer": he was praying.

The person behind or in front of him, who repeatedly stretched out, then retracted his arms, rather like a rower, to underscore his lip movements, laughed heartily during the similarly rapid rhythmic pauses in his silent tirade, his laughter, too, silent, completely silent, until the time and the moment arrived again for pushing, pulling, for opening his mouth, puckering his lips, pursing them, popping them, pressing them together, all the while shaking his head, nodding, then shaking it more vigorously, in turn: he was cursing someone; he was cursing a woman, his love, his great love.

And the person next to him, as well as the one next to the one next to him, with their almost identical mouth-opening, silent lockjaw, and identical closing, with their silent lip chorus, their mouths opened wide and promptly snapped shut: they were mocking their supervisors and bosses, by whom they'd just recently or had always been humiliated and insulted as no-goods, wimps, layabouts, dysfunctional so-and-sos (and that in times like these), born failures, congenital suckers— the one over there summarily fired only an hour ago: with their silent lip movements they were sneering all through the car, from the front to the middle to way in the back and no doubt into the next car, at those who denied their right to exist; mocking their executioners not only soundlessly but without a syllable or a word, and that would remain so and go on forever. Not once did these lips, compulsively opening and closing, form or utter a single helpful word or sound—even silently, for the sole benefit of one of these Don Quixotes—a peep of life. — "And how do you know that?" — "I know. I knew it, then and there."

Yet suddenly someone screamed, his cry bouncing off the tram's ceiling, then eyed all those around him: "I hope no one heard me." Another new phenomenon: that not only men jiggled one thigh but also women. Not a few, whether women or men, inadvertently sway-ing and bumping against the person next to them, as it were. (No, not "as it were.") And one and all, including me, were having a "bad hair day."

A number of children were on the tram. My own had long since "left home," as the expression goes, and were also no longer children, yet on this trip I still felt per-sonally responsible for the children; with amplification, so to speak, heard their cries as directed at me; I was the father whom the strange child was calling, and so urgently; it tugged at me every time.

One of the tram children was scrutinizing me from afar. He tried to catch my eye, not out of curiosity or attraction, and quickly looked away the minute he succeeded, before going back to the game of eyeing me. Independently of the child and me, something was at stake, and I felt obliged to play along. Playing a game with children I didn't know had given me special pleasure in my middle years, for it involved something significant, though of an "undetermined nature." And in those days I always won. This time I lost. For some reason the child's gaze became somber and scornful, as happens only with little children who can't talk yet, and in that moment of sudden somberness and scorn, the child turned away from me and lost interest for good in the likes of me; I could smile till the cows came home— any reconciliation was out of the question. Yes: the child had had his suspicions about me all along, and now one look had proved him right; I was found out, by a one-year-old!

But ah! there was another child, an older one, with a pad of paper on the tray table in front of him; he was drawing, surreptitiously, hiding the drawing with his hand, sketching! me! Up to now no child had ever drawn me! And his scribbling, during which he repeatedly glanced up, showed he was serious about capturing me accurately; apparently the child was discovering something about his model, never mind what.

And then another child, a girl, almost an adolescent, yet still completely childlike. This child, this very young girl, was absorbed in observing another child in the opposite row, a small child, who yesterday, or only that morning, had learned to walk, just two steps, and now, balancing on its father's knees and facing him, resisting his assistance almost irritably as it tried to add to its repertory, managed to take a third step, and finally, after a long pause, teetering and tottering, took a fourth, tumbling into the man's outstretched arms. Chortling on the child's part and clapping from the adult, and not from him alone, a scene not that uncommon, but somewhat less common in a moving streetcar.

As for me, from beginning to end I'd had my eyes on the girl across from me. She wasn't with anyone in the car, wasn't related to the man-with-baby pair. She was traveling alone. This was her first time on the new tram line, the one crusading across the Île-de-France plateau. This wasn't her area, or her country. She was a foreigner. But in the country from which she'd just arrived, yesterday, no, this very morning, she'd lived as a foreigner, foreign from earliest childhood, a foreign element in her own family, and no one and nothing was to blame, neither her mother nor her father, neither the country nor the state—yes, not even the state or its form of government. There was a difference, however: if in that country the girl, this child, had been merely "the foreigner," and nothing else, here she appeared as a friendly foreigner.

I'd never witnessed a gentler form of foreignness,

not even in some of those strangers, old or also not old, who'd lost all hope, and likewise not in some person or other, presumably well known, facing death. But this girl-child, this gentle little foreigner: she beamed—not a spark of hope, also nothing like acceptance of her fate, and certainly no "I'm looking forward to dying"—she was beaming at the sight of the other child, the beaming not emanating from her eyes or her face but from her entire body, her corporeal being: from her shoulders, her stomach, her hands in her lap. My mother, I now recalled, had told me stories from her own childhood about playing "house" in her village, making particular mention of the village-idiot girl with a speech defect, who every time roles were assigned—she wasn't allowed to join in any other games—could be heard bawling from under the cherry tree in the center of the village, "Mebedemudda!" ("*I'm* the mother!")

But no: the way the foreign girl beamed, not openly at the other child, more quietly to herself: there was nothing idiotlike about that. Or yes, there was, too. Long live such idiot girls!

Last stop. The place name doesn't matter. Somewhere in the Île-de-France. Paris spread out below in the valley of the Seine. Down there I'd continue my journey by Métro or bus. Only buses in thousands of other directions. My dear fellow passengers: almost all of them gone in a flash. I was tempted to follow one man or other, one woman or other, more or less surreptitiously, for no particular reason except maybe to see where the person might go next, riding or walking, homeward or not. Over the years it had become a kind of sport for me to trail a stranger, out of more than mere curiosity, on a hunch, and also—the decisive factor?—a sense of duty, from Métro line to Métro line, on metropolitan buses to the outskirts and then on the regional bus, and each of those sorties had afforded me richly satisfying hours or half-days, free of interactions or confrontations, and had stayed with me as a source of stories, always ready to be explored anew, far more than a mere pastime.

There were many passengers I was inclined to follow, and each of them set out in a different direction on the plateau. I decided to let it go, relieved this time of my daily guilt over dereliction of duty. That was how buoyed up I felt from the tram ride.

And that other duty, the one for whose sake I'd set out from home in the first place, my pressing duty, now even more terribly urgent than before? If I wasn't exactly heading in a direction opposite to the approximate scene of the dastardly deed committed in words against my mother, which would have been the wrong direction, I was certainly taking a detour. I'd planned, after all, to change at the tram terminal to the number such-and-such bus (a three-figure number), which had a scheduled stop right at my destination. (This thought brought to mind, who knows why, something a farmer back home had said one May morning as he set out to mow the dewy grass along a brook with his scythe; he'd commented that the conditions were "just right.")

Nonsense: I hadn't worked out or settled on any plan. I hadn't left home with a specific route or destination or indeed anything in particular in mind. Something had to happen: that was inscribed on my heart, and had set me in motion. On the other hand, yes, right: a plan did exist. It exists. But it isn't my plan, worked out by me, and wasn't, and isn't, something to be executed by me—not for anything in the world! And only now was I beginning to sense the plan, or guess what it might be. And I also knew this: heading off at first in a wrong direction was a component, a building block of the plan. "Wrong direction": more nonsense. I, we, would see.

After that I covered a long stretch on foot. — "So what about your resolution, my friend, to stick to public transportation this time, on this particular day? You and your resolutions!" — "Yes, oh my, my resolutions, part of my unfortunate tendency to jump the gun. Because now the plan came into focus, and all resolutions, mine I mean, fell by the wayside."

For quite a while I wasn't conscious of walking, and the direction hardly mattered. The only thing that accompanied me in the hour that followed, constantly pounded into me like a piece of worldly wisdom, was a song from childhood, "My hat, it has three corners / Three corners has my hat / And had it not three corners / It would not be my hat," until summoning up a fragment from Blaise Pascal's *Pensées* finally brought relief, a passage in which he comments on the four-cornered hats worn by jurists.

I was walking along roads and streets of various types, passing through several suburban developments (located on the sites of old villages), keeping for the most part to sidewalks but simply walking on the shoulder in areas that lacked them, where one settlement flowed into the next without the usual spaces in between. In my imagination I was staying on the shoulder, not wending my way around houses and the edges of squares, as was actually the case, but cutting straight across open countryside, with habitations only in the distance, following a single road that led from one unspecified locale to another on far-flung waves of asphalt. As long as I kept walking, nothing bad could happen to me and the likewise unspecified beings I cared about, and whatever was supposed to happen for one of them or another would come to pass. I imagined furthermore that with my walking, especially the way I walked, I was exemplifying something to people in the passing cars. My walking along what I imagined as the "highway"— don't criticize these imaginings—would prove infectious to the four or more people I could glimpse through the glittering car windows, prompting them some fine day, if not here and now, to emulate this intrepid walker, striding along, with or without a destination. How his trousers fluttered and flapped around his legs. How his white shirt billowed and ballooned. "What a pity"— I told myself again—"that my walking outfit isn't my grandfather's Sunday go-to-meeting suit or the classic black jacket, vest, trousers, and round hat in which journeyman carpenters once traveled the continent on foot from north to south."

When I managed to see inside a car now and then, however, I thought I could tell that if the sight of a pedestrian provided any example it was more off-putting than appealing; the glazed eyes showed not a flicker of desire to be tramping along that way. When I glanced down at my feet—"just keep going, no matter what; don't fall out of character!"—I noticed that I was wearing socks from two altogether different pairs. "So what: that's part of the game. The avenger with unmatched socks." And what image did this walker on the shoulder of the *grande route* present from behind? He made an impression, though apparently one very different from my daydream: a car, a compact model, passed me, then pulled over onto the shoulder, or what I imagined as such, and an elderly man poked his head out of the half-open window, and in the self-amplifying voice of a do-gooder offered me a ride. And my regret afterward, as I remembered the intense disappointment in his eyes, that I'd turned him down; this would be the last time he invited a stranger into his car; for the foreseeable future he wouldn't do a favor for anyone.

And as for me, enough cross-country walking: "This has to be the last time!" And what was special about what's now turned out to have been "the last time": as I was walking, in midstream (but wasn't it "in midstream" from beginning to end? — Don't go all pedantic on me! — Who's being pedantic?), as I was walking, in mid-stream I was suddenly overcome by hunger, a wild, all-consuming hunger, the very essence of hunger, without any tangible object, let alone an edible one, a hunger that began or ended not in my stomach or in my bowels but in my forehead—away with the Tolstoyan visor—under my skull, as gnawing as any hunger could be, but impossible to assuage and certainly impossible to sate. And step after step, as I strode on and on, this burning yet vague hunger acquired not an object but a direction toward a place, a specific one.

By the next available taxi—in a pinch I would have chartered a helicopter—I was now driven to Port-Royal-des-Champs, the site of the abandoned abbey and the remaining ruins, where, in a narrow side-valley in the southwest of the Île-de-France, wooded and swampy then as now, Blaise Pascal (and, after him, Jean Racine) had spent his schoolboy years. In the past I'd made a point of paying an annual visit to the spot, and always in the month of May.

A long time had passed since I'd been in Port-Royal-in-the-Fields. And now it was May, the first week of May, and this particular day was the right one. Previously it had been especially the surrounding area that spoke to me, but even more so the route one took to get there, which was long, crossing plateaus and valleys carved out by brooks; but most of all I looked forward each time to leaving, walking backward for a few minutes, one more time, "and one more time." Now, however, I was hungering for Port-Royal-de-Pascal.

The taxi driver cleared off the passenger seat for me, and during the long cross-country ride, as he told me his story, I suddenly thought I recognized his voice and involuntarily called him by name, in a spontaneous exclamation. In his day, or ours, he'd been a singer one often heard on the radio, popular less for his own songs—of which he'd written only two or three, or maybe only one—than for his French versions of blues and ballad songs with English lyrics. His hits, or *tubes* (Fr.), he owed to a British singer, as young as he was back then, and now—*"Que Dieu le protège!"*—as old as the two of us, the taxi driver and his passenger, and still our hero, without needing to have died a hero's death: Eric Burdon. When it came to hits and songs, as well as poems, I usually retained at most one line or half a line (excepting, strangely, the words of the Austrian national anthem, of which I knew an entire stanza by heart). But I knew (and know) the text of Eric Burdon's ballad "When I Was Young" from the first line to the last, and could even sing it, provided I was alone, though not, of course, in the "blackest blues voice of any white person," which was what people said Eric Burdon had, but at least, or so I liked to think, in English with a vaguely Slavic accent. But now, on the outskirts of Port-Royal-des-Champs, we launched into "When I Was Young" / "Kad Sam Bio Mlad" / "Quand j'étais jeune" as a duet, in three versions at once, as it were. We sang the line

"I believed in fellow man . . . when I was young" in the original, bawling it in unison.

Then we sat, with a glimpse of the famous roof of the Port-Royal barn shimmering bronze through blooming chestnut trees, on the terrace of the restaurant called Au Chant des Oiseaux (The Birdsong), which had just opened under new management for the umpteenth time—"good luck!"—the taxi driver and I, each of us having offered at the identical moment to treat the other, as the only guests, and not just since that morning; the cigarette butt in a glass on the next table looked to have been there quite a while. The man's reason for driving a taxi in his golden years was not that he was short of money—money was no problem. He was bored sitting around the house, and even more bored tending his good-sized plot of land. Hadn't Pascal, way back in the seventeenth century, equated boredom with death, in its most ignominious form: "withering up"? And besides, the former singer loved to drive: even back in the day he, the bandleader or lead singer, had insisted on climbing into the driver's seat between concerts. And nowadays he had a particular yen to drive the Bentley (or whatever his car was) around his ancestral area, the Île-de-France, by day and even more by night. What a joy to drive, first with, then without, his passenger—who'd got out somewhere to cover the last stretch to his home on foot in that post-midnight hour—to drive, till the sky showed a hint of gray, along the almost deserted streets of the départements of Essonne, Vale-de-Marne, Val-d'Oise, with not a soul in sight, and on from Pointoise to Conflans-Sainte-Honorine, from Meaux to Guermantes, from Bièvres to Bourg-la-Reine. In parting, we gave each other a hug.

The grounds of Port-Royal were open. But for quite a while I remained the only visitor. From years of experience I knew that few visitors came; not much was left to see, and in the Rhodon Valley hardly a stone remained of the abbey in which the nuns and their pupils Pascal and Racine had lived. But no: there they were, the centuries-old stone steps leading up the steep slope between the abbey's grounds down in the meadows and the outbuildings up on the plateau, which were almost entirely intact. As I did every time, I mounted the stairs, counting the steps, and did the same on the way down, and as always happened, I ended up with a different number. Had the hunger, still burning in the middle of my forehead as I stood outside the gates, subsided once I entered? Wasn't I in danger, right here in Pascal country, of being overcome by the boredom he describes? Oh no: the hunger remained acute, intensified now by perplexity. "I have to make up my mind soon!" I shouted into the deserted memorial park (or did I only imagine myself shouting?). "I need advice!" (True: I couldn't really have shouted; I would have heard the echo from the Port-Royal slope.)

Where to turn? Where would it reveal itself, the one

and only advice- or oracle-station before which I could plant myself, so to speak—no, not "so to speak"! However and wherever I stumbled, slid, tripped, fell (on my behind or some other body part), back and forth, up and down, crisscrossing the so-to-speak sacred precincts of Port-Royal-des-Champs — enough of your damned "so to speak"! — nowhere did the message reach me: It's here / there! Now! This is it!

Many, many a time in my life, when I'd been searching for something, fervently but not desperately, and was almost at the point (desperate is desperate and means "dead"—and what does "at the point" mean?) of giving up once and for all, I'd come upon what I was looking for, and always unexpectedly; though I couldn't count on it; no question of trusting the world or existence to come through for me!

But on this particular day it worked. In one of the most out-of-the-way corners of the grounds—not a glimmer or shimmer of "precincts"—trapped in an unending thicket of blackberry canes, after what seemed like interminable attempts to free myself (see above), I unexpectedly, after raising my knee one last time, stumbled out into what had probably been a clearing once but in the meantime had become almost entirely overgrown, with the exception of a silted-up pond and a section of retaining wall. I didn't take in the whole picture, the entire scene, until a bit later; the first thing my eye lit on was a detail—that, too, a familiar experience. Some words had been scratched into one of the wall-stones, with a nail or some other implement that had come to hand, and no, the inscription wasn't hundreds of years old, but also not from my, from our, present, though it looked as if it hadn't been there long. And I promptly read the words off the stone; no need to puzzle them out: TODAY 8 MAY 1945—BELLS PEALING VICTORY (*translated from the French*).

This was it, the spot. Now I had it, my place, my go-to place! Finally I was back at Port-Royal. "Thank you for coming back." A raven in the crest of an oak tree squawked out a greeting, and bowed and scraped to accompany it. And a very special rustling passed through the May foliage.

I settled down on the bank of the pond, my gaze fixed on the few bog-black whirlpools, and among them, half buried in the muck and forming a rhythmic line, as if they were remnants of piles, what seemed to be charred tree stumps, likewise bog-black. Unlike the war's-end inscription, these poked up as if from the depths of centuries, apparently as hard as gravel or flint, reminiscent of the piles in the Venice lagoon that marked the navigable channels, and I decreed that as a schoolboy in Port-Royal young Blaise Pascal had seen them when they were still intact, and not coal-black at all. From where could bells have been heard pealing on that eighth day of May in 1945, announcing to the Rhodon Valley and to the whole Île-de-France plateau the final collapse of the Third Reich? Those could only be the bells—two? three?—of Saint-Lambert, farther downstream in the valley, the church in whose cemetery the nuns accused of heresy, Pascal's teachers, lay buried in a mass grave.

At my feet, half sunk in the mud, a weathered pencil, and lying next to it—"What in the world is that?"—a darning needle spotted with rust. (Only the obligatory third object was missing—but never mind!) Had pencils even existed in Pascal's time, or styluses of any kind? I decreed: yes. The stylus worked, and I stowed it away. And the needle? Rusty or not: it pricked. Tucked into a safe place with the pencil.

Without thinking I rooted around in my canvas bag for my small, much abridged version of the fragmentary *Pensées*. But hadn't I decided not to take along anything resembling a book on this particular day? And rightly so. I was relieved. Closing my eyes, I felt at that moment as though I could also hardly hear anything, aside from distant wind, not up here on the plateau but down in the valley of the vanished Port-Royal abbey, a valley wind. "Close up the gates of your senses!" — "They're closed."

To be considered: without their square hats and robes four times too wide, the magistrates couldn't put anything over on the world. But the world can't resist a spectacle. If they truly had justice on their side, the magistrates would have no need to wear those hats. The gravitas conferred by their expertise would be all the authority they needed. But since their expertise is merely imagined, those gentlemen of the law must appeal to

the imagination, by means of which they come to actually wield authority. All authorities wear disguises. Only
the kings of olden times had no need to disguise themselves. They didn't don a particular costume to appear
mighty, might personified. King Louis, not the four-
teenth, and certainly not the fifteenth, but the much
earlier Louis—king and crusader—almost always wore a
gray-green doublet that rendered him more inconspicu-
ous than the lowliest page, and on his head, if anything,
a cloth cap of a nondescript color, easy to mistake for
his hair—or was the cap worn by young Louis XI, whose
head often ached, made of wool, knitted by his beloved
Marguerite de Navarre?

But now the kings of old are dead and gone, and
the rest of us need disguises and the trappings of the
imagination. And it's the imagination, not reason, that
brings forth the appearance of beauty, of happiness,
and of justice. Yes, "imagined justice": that's what's at
issue here and now, and what do I care whether the law,
justice codified, is on my side or not? In my imagination
there's no justice on earth now without violence, which
means the law of the sword, opposed to what is seemingly the highest justice, in essence the highest form
of injustice, and not only in the case of "my mother."
Summum jus, summa injuria. The law of the sword: true
justice! The perpetrator I'm after is one of those from
the other side of the river. If she were from this side, it
wouldn't be just of me to punish her, and I would be the
super-perpetrator. But since I imagine her as living on

the far side of the water, the highest form of justice is to kill her, one way or the other. If there were still a kingdom that recognized me: ah, its obligation, not mine. But where are they, the kingdoms that recognize me?

Preoccupied with these thoughts, I had long since slid backward off the remnant of wall and was lying in the grass. And I must have fallen asleep. I had a dream. It was a dream such as I hadn't had since my youth: it felt as real as anything I'd ever experienced when awake, including when I was at my most alert, with the exception, perhaps, of those moments when I was shaken, shaken to the core. What happened in the dream initially recapitulated something that had actually taken place once between my mother and me. But how and in what form that occurrence was repeated in the dream! How . . . how . . . incredibly real. Out of the blue—or that's how it seems to me as I record that mother-son scene in writing—breaching the often peaceful, indeed intimate domestic relationship the two of us enjoyed, the adolescent had asked her—not yet forty and still the village beauty, and, when the occasion called for it, also the beauty in the nearest town—why she hadn't resisted that criminal regime in any way, no, in her own way. It came out as a question, yet it was a reproach, sudden and fierce, generated in part by sheer obstinacy, I suppose, but chiefly by my inability to comprehend, and the rage I still feel today. I could have challenged someone else in the family, and outside of the family, too. But because I couldn't think of anyone else, the victim of all of my outbursts, at least in those days, was my poor innocent mother. She didn't reply, just wrung her hands. And then she wept, without a word, wailed and sobbed, as her would-be judge just stood there. And that sobbing must have gone on forever.

Up to that point my dream reproduced the scene exactly, except that I saw it as if in SuperCinemaScope, without me: my mother alone on the dream screen, in an enormous close-up. But then, after a momentary blackout, my mother's face again, even more monumental, if possible, planet-sized: my mother's face in death, no, after death, ageless, and somehow alive as never before. It was she, my mother, and it was a stranger, a terrible one. Or the other way around: a terrible stranger stared at me from a single eye, open wide, the other having seemingly disappeared into a large swelling, and that was my mother. She'd told me once that as a child she'd been stung on the forehead by a hornet, between the eyes, which had left her blind for a whole week. The face I saw now had no background, was surrounded by deep blackness, against which it appeared as white as chalk. In another story from her childhood she'd gone to look for a lost calf and got tangled in a thorn bush, remaining stuck there for a day and a night.

This mother's dream face was no longer that of the storyteller who, in the middle of the most earnest and heartrending family tales, would dish up a detail that gave the listener something to laugh at, whereupon my mother, in her typical mixture of embarrassment and pride at what she'd pulled off, would giggle along with me. "Storyteller—seed-sower": that was over, gone for good, the dream said. The face belonged to an avenger. It cried out, even if not a word was spoken during the entire dream: nothing but that eye blazing at me, crying out for revenge.

While she was alive, and long before she sank into depression, I was always afraid for her, without reason, for no reason at all. Now I was afraid of her for the first time. The revenge involved me, her son. Revenge had to be taken, on me, and me alone. And revenge had already been taken. This face, appearing, emerging abruptly, from amid the blackest black, tearless and eternally beyond tears: that already constituted the act of revenge. And the reason? Another of those stupid questions we ask ourselves upon waking up. In the dream it was crystal clear: this avenger didn't need a reason. It was as it was.

On the other hand, a dream like that in which nothing happened, with nothing but that face expressing silently what it had to say, gave a person no choice but to wake up at once. And then it was urgent that I get away from the place with that message scratched into the wall about bells pealing to mark the war's end, a message historic, yet more than seven decades later as fresh as if from yesterday—to flee from history into the present, and that also meant, and meant above all, into Blaise Pascal's present. To his room in the museum?

No, scrambling over boulders and through brush toward that intact barn roof.

Up there, under a blooming elderberry bush, I found a bench; the barn—long since used only for performances of plays and concerts—at my back. The spot offered a view down into the valley, but not of the abbey grounds, the chapel, and the dove tower; the May foliage blocked that view, and the hundred-odd stone steps scaling the slope were also out of sight; before my eyes I had only nature. And that was how it was meant to be. I alternated between staring straight ahead at the infinitely delicate creamy elderberry blossoms, almost close enough to touch and swaying in the May afternoon breeze, up and down, back and forth, and gazing over the tip of this natural pagoda into the heavens. Audience time. Waiting quietly. And then the moment had come.

True, my friend: in the century past the world came crashing down, indeed several times. Doomsday. And that was the case in all previous human centuries, with each crash taking a different form.

But enough of doomsdays of one kind or another. Back to one of my key concepts: "imagination." I would replace this word now with another: "appearances": a word whose German form—*Schein*—has a number of meanings, both positive and, above all, negative. But only one interests me, the sole positive meaning, that special one—listen up!—the meaning that adds something essential, a life-enhancing element: appearances as an additive. Possible synonyms: "light"? "glow"? "shimmer"? "halo"? "glory"? "heavenly"? "terrestrial"?— I'm serious, friend, so you should stay serious, too, as serious as you are—you in particular. For the seriousness we both feel should form part of our discussion of appearances as an add-on. So: the appearances I'm talking about are appearances, and no other word will do. Appearances aren't "imagination," and are also not produced out of nothing by the "power of the imagination." Appearances exist for themselves and by themselves, as matter, substance, original substance, the substance of substance. And appearances can't be analyzed, can't be studied by any of the sciences, nor can they be quantified, in terms of length, breadth, height, or volume, by means of mathematics, the most luminous of the sciences, and the most false—yet my chosen science, my first . . . Yes, study what can be studied, and revere in silence that which can't be studied. — Appearances as the secret of the beautiful? — Leave "the beautiful" out of it! Away with that word, and enough of beauty, whether with or without quotation marks. It's not beauty that's the origin of the terrible, as Rilke would have it, but the search for beauty, being on the lookout for it, listening for it, lusting after it, wanting to possess it. There's no longing more wrongheaded than the longing for beauty! All the misery in the world comes from human beings' inability to forget the old wives' tale of beauty.

All the deserts and badlands of beauty. By contrast, the springs, brooks, streams, and oceans of appearances! The Pacific of appearances. Without appearances: me and my nothingness. Appearances equal life. We've set sail. *Nous sommes embarqués!* — But since your childhood days here in Port-Royal, didn't you spare no effort to be "nothing," "my nothingness," "the weak one"? — Remember: "As I write down my thought, it sometimes escapes me; but this makes me recall my weakness, which I constantly forget. This is as instructive to me as my forgotten thought, for I strive only to know my nothingness." — Hey, look at that: the white cloud on the horizon, as in the painting by Poussin in which God the Father lies on his stomach while creating Paradise. And on the opposite horizon the other strip of May clouds, which couldn't be any whiter, a vast field in the heavens, furrowed in a soft pattern as if freshly harrowed. Are harrows still used in farming, whether drawn by oxen, horses, or tractors? — They are.

As it happened I then encountered a second visitor to Port-Royal-des-Champs, someone I'd never have expected to see in this place. Like voices on the railway station's loudspeaker, but softer and also more personal, I suddenly heard from above and to one side an unfamiliar voice, and, also in contrast to the railway announcements, one that asked, "May I join you?" When I looked up, I saw a familiar figure standing next to me, right there in front of the bench, as motionless as if he'd been standing there for a while. Now he stepped back a pace and let me have a good look at him, and finally I recognized him.

It was someone from my area, though not from the immediate neighborhood. He lived a few side streets away. Nonetheless I saw him often, usually from a distance, when he came out of the railway station in early evening and set out for his house or apartment while I sat on the terrace of the Three Stations, letting the day wind down (or begin to wind up). As if blind to anyone or anything, he would strut straight across the square, and every time I thought, "another bigwig." From the bar's owner, who knew everyone in the area, I learned that he was a judge, a judge of the court in nearby Versailles, though for minor cases; earlier he would probably have been called a "rocket-docket judge" or "police magistrate." It also happened that our paths crossed once, or rather I intentionally crossed his path, passing too close to him for a moment, which meant he couldn't avoid registering my presence and swept me with the quick glance that expresses, "So what does *he* want?", just as my brother, when I confronted him one time, with my mother's backing, brushed me off with a scornful "What do *you* want?"

No question about it: the person who now matter-of-factly took a seat beside me under the blooming elderberry was the same one I'd felt like giving a good kick when I saw him in our neighborhood. He was astonished to run into me in the solitude of Port-Royal-des-Champs, and I felt the same about him. Astonished and pleased, as was he.

After that he did all the talking. He'd come on his bicycle, as he did almost every weekend, the trip here and back taking all day. The way he was dressed helped explain in part why I hadn't recognized him at first: rather than cycling gear, he was wearing an old suit, with a bicycle clip still clinging to one of the pant legs. The judge was especially enamored of the tiles on the roof of the Port-Royal barn; he could never get enough of their yellowish orange glow, he said; as a child he'd squatted for hours on the rim of an enormous clay pit, and the sight he'd had into the depths was recapitulated, inverted, in the Port-Royal roof. For his retirement he'd bought a cottage in Buloyer, the next village over, and from its highest window he had an unobstructed view westward to the barn roof of Port-Royal. Besides, this was one of the best mushrooming areas in the entire Île-de-France, though today he hadn't had much luck; it was probably too late for morels, and too early for the unique St. George's mushrooms, which don't taste like ordinary mushrooms but are simply "delectable," and also, as studies have shown, good for one's coronary arteries. Whereupon he showed me his almost empty cap, whereupon I reciprocated by pointing out a dazzlingly white, many-headed army of those very May knights he'd just praised so highly—with my wholehearted agreement; they were peeping out of the light shade cast by a maple tree. I'd spotted them immediately, but picking them would have violated the pledge I'd made to myself to refrain on this particular day from my usual follies.

With a precious harvest safely stashed in his hat, the judge rejoined me on the bench, but after that he spoke mostly to himself. It was as if I didn't exist for him, though not in the same way as when our paths had crossed on the good old square outside the station: "How I hate imposing sentences. Judge: what an impossible profession. Pure presumption. On the other hand, Lucifer was actually the light bringer. Being a judge: never again. A special hell reserved for us judges. But there's one penalty, a single one among all those the law allows, that I would impose with conviction, would recognize as necessary, as particularly urgent right now, as a form of deterrence. And that's the penalty for malicious litigation or abuse of the legal process, an offense for which nowadays hardly any perpetrator is forced to accept responsibility, let alone penalized. Yet as I see it, people who abuse their legal rights aren't just the majority among all the lawbreakers and scofflaws; they also inflict one injustice after another on those whom they constantly, day after day, flog with their rights, and against whom they assert those rights—and this is the essence of process abuse!—needlessly, groundlessly, senselessly, simply out of malice, thereby causing their victims one misfortune after another, harm upon harm. Rights abuse has become its own religion, a form of idolatry, perhaps the very last one: exercising and exaggerating one's own rights vis-à-vis someone else as proof of one's existence. I beat everyone over the head with my rights, therefore I am. Only that guarantees my existence. That's all that guarantees their existence and allows them to feel like themselves, these people who violate with impunity the prohibition on malicious prosecution or abuse of process. Violators of the law? Killers of the law! And killers of more than just those particular legal principles. We should establish special prisons for these modern evildoers. And then wait and see what happens when the inmates play poker from cell to cell with their marked rights. Ahoy!—rights abuse, the only offense for which there's no statute of limitations, and also not a single extenuating circumstance! But these aren't the only cases that reveal that there's no such thing as a sense of community anymore. There's no general consensus, and certainly no *volonté générale*. Maybe there never was, but the word became flesh and prevailed among us and over us. No more community. But perhaps that will bring about the great liberation."

The judge gradually returned to his senses, though the movements of his lips suggested that in his head his lecture on the law was continuing. Finally he brought the edge of his hand down on the bench, as if he were a symphonic conductor marking the beat in a rehearsal, and as he looked at me and laughed, his whole face lit up: because the entire thing had been a private joke, or because he'd got something off his chest? Hard to tell. Whatever the case, we sat there side by side for a while longer, he leaning back so he could gaze at the barn roof,

I captivated by the steady stream of elderberry blossoms drifting down before me. Not another word exchanged. And yet we now had a bond by virtue of having met in that place, unexpectedly, and that bond would endure.

My momentary thought: Might something similar have taken place with the woman who'd slandered my mother if she'd crossed my path in this remote spot? A mutual rapprochement, a reconciliation? No way! Any such thing was out of the question, no matter where, no matter when. But no revenge would have been enacted here either, not here: the place was off limits, a place of refuge, and not because this Port-Royal-des-Champs was special (which it was) but because the woman and I would have found ourselves face-to-face without a plan.

In parting and as an "*au revoir!*" I wanted to surprise the judge with a trick we children had learned back in the village: blowing into the hollow stem of a dandelion to produce a prolonged deep drone, or more of a buzz. But he turned out to be the one to surprise me. He picked several such stems at once, of differing thicknesses, bunched them together, stuck them between his judge's lips, and look! no, listen! a sound issued forth like a many-voiced fanfare, mixed with the notes of a bagpipe, no, not that word, a cornemuse, with undertones of a bullhorn: a few moments of music such as I, and, as I again decreed, the whole world had never heard before.

In the end the judge proclaimed, in a voice softened by his music making, "And yet: long live the law! Yes, the law as a source of delight, a very special delight, to be found, for instance, in the eyes of children. They don't judge—they decide. The fourth power. Yet who wields this power?" And after a pause: "Look at that: the pattern of the roof tiles on the old barn suggests an alternative map of the world!" And after another pause, with a glance at me as if he were in the know: "You have something serious ahead of you. May my good wishes go with you."

At the very end the judge even began to stammer, which only reinforced my trust in him, as had always happened to me with stammerers. And then one of the few utterances I could make out: "I'm an orphan!" ("*Je suis un orphelin!*")

As I departed from Port-Royal—doing some walking backward again—I felt the urge to pledge something to the light shining through the trees—except that I didn't know what to pledge.

Heading east toward the bus stop on the path that ran along the edge of the woods, out of the more or less clear blue sky I suddenly felt pressed for time. That sensation could come over me any day of the week, and always without a particular reason, sneaking up on me. Usually the sensation just grazed me, then released me, banished by the counterspell of reason. On this day, too, I tried appealing to reason, reminding myself, "There's still plenty of time till evening, and in May it doesn't get dark till late," but the time crunch kept me in its grip, especially in my throat. The time crunch made it hard to breathe, and it didn't help when reason tried to calm me by suggesting that my agony resulted from a hallucination that had me imagining I was heading east and toward darkness.

This kind of time crunch—manifesting itself today, as always, on the verge of late afternoon, which suddenly seemed impossible to reach—usually ushered in a stretch of time and distance, sometimes shorter, sometimes longer, during which I yearned for nothing more fervently than to be spared the company of other humans. And so it was this time. Except that on my way to the bus stop, when I needlessly found myself from one step to the next in a tearing hurry, my literally chronic, i.e., ephemeral, "temporary" aversion to others turned into full-blown misanthropy, taking the form of mortal enmity, and reason—mine, that is—proved helpless against it, even though it whispered to me after every few hectic steps that the minute I encountered even a single person in flesh and blood, no matter what flesh and blood, even evil in person, my murderous rage would promptly revert to my ordinary late-afternoon avoidance of others, which made me lower or turn my head so as not to look at the other person. "Just wait for the next person sharing this path: you'll silently beg his forgiveness for the hatred you're feeling, even if he's walking three pit bulls."

Not another soul turned up as I hurtled along in the grip of my time crunch. And that was fine with me. I actually reveled in my rage and my hostility toward my fellow humans. Also, and most importantly, the time crunch itself disappeared. A shooting range must have been located in the woods along which I was walking, for at intervals I could hear the dull thud of bullets. Arrows whirred through the air and vibrated sonorously as they struck the target, or less sonorously if they missed. I eard the buzzing and banging of crossbows. And every time the shooter was me; me, me, and me again. And the child's slingshot lying beside the path, its bands badly frayed: that was mine. So restring it! But what a pity, an eternal pity, that this misanthrope's path was so short, hardly a dozen bowshots or at most two dozen stone's throws long.

On the other hand, the more I relished being the sworn enemy of all mankind, the more queasy I felt. How disturbing that I had no idea what was going on in the world at the moment. The fact was, I didn't merely have a bad conscience about being out of touch since that morning and by now almost the whole day; I saw my habit of ignoring information, no matter what, as utterly irresponsible and a form of guilt, an acute form. Why had I taken no interest in the latest disasters, mass shootings, assassinations? What if the world was no longer standing and all this merely a dying glow? And look: the billboards erected along the turnoff to the bus stop and halfway through the village in preparation for the European elections: not a single face on a poster, all the surfaces bare!—But there: a May bug under the cherry tree by the sidewalk, almost as big as my thumb, with the bright saw-blade pattern on the sides of its shell: dead, frozen in the May night, and there: another, and that one is scrabbling along, is alive! So contrary to what you hear, May bugs haven't gone extinct. Information! Good news!

Waiting for the bus in a windowless concrete shelter on the side of yet another Île-de-France highway, just outside the village. A young couple were standing there, silent, the man's arms drooping, his wife a small step away from him, their bodies not touching except that she repeatedly brushed her hand down his back from top to bottom. That gesture was new to me, at any rate not recognizable as a caress. Or perhaps it was one after all, and this caress had become customary in the world, and not merely the western world, while I was sleeping and dreaming in Pascalian seclusion. And it felt as though I'd spent years in Port-Royal during this one day.

The couple left without wasting a glance on me. Or thus: from the beginning they hadn't registered my presence. That suggested they hadn't been waiting for a bus at all. So was this stop no longer in use, and the bus line I'd used in years past no longer in operation? But no: on the wall I saw the current bus schedule, and it included weekend service.

I, who'd only recently been suffering from an intense time crunch, now found time dragging. I imagined it came from my still going unnoticed. That typically happened when I encountered highway bicyclists, especially those riding in groups, arrayed in their cycling gear, complete with helmets, and preoccupied with their conversations—they had to shout over the hum of their wheels. From the cars, too, their numbers barely increasing now in late afternoon, not a single gaze rested on or brushed me; if the occupants had eyes for anything, it was the road, or, if there were several of them, each other. Yet I pictured myself as a striking figure, in my three-part, grayish-black Dior suit, my wide-brimmed Borsalino with a buzzard feather stuck in the band, and my dark glasses, as I sat there alone on the moldering bench in the bus shelter.

I stepped out of the shelter and posted myself by the road. Not that I wished a bolt of lightning would strike me from on high. But for one long moment I was actually ready for that, so intensely did I long for a proof of my existence. I squatted on a curbstone, choosing one much larger and thicker than the others in the row, also out of alignment and almost overgrown with May nettles, which have a piercing sting all their own. When I pulled up a couple of the plants with my bare hands, stinging myself on purpose (it felt good at first), I noticed on the stone—which was not concrete like the rest but granite—an incised crown, clearly not from today or yesterday. I carefully traced its mossy outlines, first with my fingernails and then with the miniature Saracen dagger, hardly the length of my middle finger, that I'd slipped into my pocket as usual. Then I scratched my legs several times to call any observer's attention to what I'd found, as if by pulling back a curtain: "Just look at this, will you: a curbstone from royal times, and the idiot for the day squatting on it, as if it were reserved for him, and see the mad fellow on his royal stone performing a dance without raising his buttocks so much as an inch; see him dancing a seat dance, long out of fashion, by the side of our former royal road, and on the sharp edges of his throne cliff, too!"

But no one paid attention, to me or to anyone or anything else. Better to be convicted and consigned to the dust heap than to be ignored. Every man for himself, and that applied not only to the vehicles and their occupants but also to the one group of hikers, an individual group, so to speak, old folks and young, with or without hiking sticks, who passed by, shouting cheerfully to each other without wasting a glance on me, the curbstone sitter, and likewise to the two or three solo hikers, engrossed in their trail maps as they trudged along.

Yet I had a responsibility toward them. It was urgent that I see them all, those in vehicles as much as those on foot, driving and walking beneath the sky of the Île-de-France, and not only the Île-de-France—a responsibility I didn't manage to fulfill, not in the slightest. A very young man, seemingly coming from afar, from the bright west, hauling an enormous suitcase, one without wheels, eventually approached me, with the light shining directly on him, so I couldn't make out his face until he was passing, almost bumping into me—he, too, overlooking me, not on purpose—for him I didn't exist—he had a very youthful face, and at the same time a face, what a rarity, from olden times. I turned away from him to look tentatively toward the zenith—and he, meanwhile, the near-child with that face from bygone times, the days of Louis the Crusader or of Percival, walked along as if there were no sky.

But then: in my after-gaze, over my shoulder, at the back of his head and torso: When was the last time someone like him had walked along beneath such a sky? And into the evening and far into the night I was to see not a few people driving, walking, standing, sitting, lying beneath that sky.

During the whole time I waited by the highway for the bus, there had reached me from the village, or from a single house, sounds and voices such as one hears only from a festive gathering, and I'd thought: "Too early for a festival, at least for me. Spare me your May Day celebrations. Let my festivity, a revenge fest, celebrated by revenge light, wait for evening, wait till night!"

Now, however, I wished one of the participants in the festivity would find his way to me on the royal curbstone and invite me to join them—I wished that, even though I'd conceived this day as one when wishing would do no good. In particular, a woman's voice coming from the site of the gathering made me prick up my ears, especially her laugh: at times cheerful, then dismissive, then even high-spirited, but at the same time like the laugh of my mother, who laughed despair-ingly at everything and everyone around her, and above all at herself. — A laugh on the verge of despair, yet also a festive laugh? — That's how it was. That's how it is— retracing phantoms of my mother over decades past.

The bus at last, flashing its headlights from afar as if for me personally. Earlier in the day most of the buses I'd encountered had been nearly empty, but as I got on, I saw that this one was veritably bursting with passengers, most of them with foreign faces, more foreign both individually and en masse hard to imagine, and at the same time almost alarmingly familiar at first glance. Yes, maybe this was a bus for farmworkers, the kind I knew from Spain, packed with *labradores*? And at once my nose was filled with the scent of onions, oranges, corn on the cob, and, most prominently, fresh cilantro.

But no, these broad faces, all resembling each other, weren't those of farmworkers. At most one ancient fellow among them had been that long ago, back home in Andalusia or Romania. Yet from the front to the very back the passengers were the children and grandchildren of *labradores*, whether Spanish, North African, or Balkan. Except that they no longer worked others' land, and perhaps hadn't inherited any notion of land and farming, had lived since birth here on the plateau of the Île-de-France, and had become salesgirls, waiters, household employees, dog trainers, and dry cleaners, and the late-afternoon bus was bringing them home to their apartments in one of the new scattered developments or another.

From station to station more passengers got off, and the image of them that's stayed with me is that of villagers, especially village women, returning from a holiday outing; they could have come from the village where I grew up. And as the bus emptied out, a few faces revealed themselves as completely different in an indefinable way, also not related to their age. Each of the few passengers still on the bus was reading, though only one was reading a book. Otherwise they were reading—a remarkable but also familiar sight—maps that they'd unfolded, for now they had enough elbow room; not local trail maps but largish maps, showing entire countries; and wasn't one person reading a map of the world? Yes, and I even saw one passenger studying an astronomical atlas.

But I couldn't take my eyes off the young black woman sitting with a book by the window in the very back. At first all I noticed was her face, which was evenly black from top to bottom, her individual features impossible to make out, almost ghostly, even ominous by contrast with the May landscape passing by outside, greener than green now in this interval between afternoon and evening. What awaited us, aside from my own concerns? (As an adolescent I'd come up with a story once when I was riding home from school on the evening bus: next to the driver a madman suddenly popped up, shouting, "I am God!" and seizing the steering wheel plunged himself "along with all of us" into the abyss.) Only after a while did I notice the African woman's arm, braced on her raised knee, and her hand holding the book; no, what I was seeing was the opposite of a ghost or a frightening image. And that came from the whiteness of the book's pages, which flashed as they were turned or whenever the reader's hand moved in a seemingly involuntary gesture.

It wasn't unusual for me to see strangers reading this way, and it seemed to happen more often now than before, or perhaps with time I'd developed a particular awareness of various kinds of readers, and every time I saw them I was at the point—which is where I remained—of asking them what, which book, they were reading "so beautifully." In the case of this reader, however, it didn't even occur to me to wonder about the title. I didn't need to know, certain as I was that she was reading the quintessential book, from the series "book of books." All my life, though always exclusively in the context of nature, I'd experienced three colors that came together to form an image of peace: the sky, a mountain, a river (classic) as "flag colors," colors of a peace flag: here, in the green outside the bus window, the white of the book's pages, and the black-on-black of the reader, I realized for the first time that such flag colors didn't have to come from nature. And I imagined her reading continuing one day in deepest Africa. One hand yielded to the other in turning the page, and likewise one finger to the next.

The final bus stop had once been a railway station, in one of the side valleys in the Île-de-France carved by a tributary of the Seine. But the bus ride, in the end almost a trip, was meant to continue until the conclusion of the story, into the evening and then on into night, if not with buses from the same line then with so-called shuttle buses. The rail network around Paris was being completely rebuilt, and that had ushered in the "shuttle-bus era," with the buses using the railway stations as their destinations, and between stations, because they couldn't follow the rails, having to take enormous detours that added greatly to the travel time, looping on secondary roads through areas the passengers would ordinarily never have seen, repeatedly approaching the borders of the Île-de-France and in some places—of which more later—going well beyond them.

That suited me just fine. After the brief time-crunch episode, I now felt I had time in abundance, as if that were also a particular law of spiritual nature; at any rate, I declared it to be that. And in fact I experienced what occurred during that shuttle-bus trip—including the sad and bad occurrences—as time in abundance, time as a benevolent god, without thought for what I had in mind or what awaited me.

Loop after loop, on those enormous detours, transported hither and thither, I felt at the same time as if I were rambling along, one step after the other, from happening to happening, from image to image, with the plateau bouncing underfoot; as if I'd stopped again and again, sat down on a bench, entered an abandoned church that I'd glimpsed as we drove past. A shuttle-bus epic! "Where art thou, Homer of the shuttle buses?" On the other hand: how hard the seats were compared to those of regular buses. What a rumbling over the road compared to the usual purring that lulled one into a doze. What a jolt from even the smallest pothole. But wasn't that part of the epic?

All the footpaths wending their way among single-family and high-rise apartment houses, the edges dotted with daisies, the only flowers. An older man and a woman of the same age at the entrance to a low-income housing complex, the woman digging around in the man's deep coat pockets for the key. A boy slapping his mother in the face. All the people rushing back and forth—who was chasing them? And there: me as a child—look at that cowlick, and those chubby cheeks! And what a racket that dog's making—and in between a sound like the whimpering of a newborn. And lo and behold: there he is, the one we'd all assumed was dead, the village idiot from back home, as casual as you please, as if it were no big deal—except that in the meantime he's grown a beard—ah, meantime!

Wrangling on the sidewalk: someone's bumped the person next to him with his computer backpack, and the bumpee is retaliating with his fists.

So many children, who, when you stare at them, especially from a distance, take cover as if they were doing something wrong—yet they're just playing, like those two over there with the metal box.

See that old lady standing in front of the bench,

and standing and standing, saying to herself, "Sit!" and again "Sit!"

And the happenings observed along the hundreds of detour loops: the man on our outward trip squatting at a loss beside his tools, spread out on the side of the road, and on the return trip he's still squatting there. The man whose entire body quivers holds out his quivering hand to someone trying to give him a light. The man tattooed from head to foot, with paler than pale fingertips that he's gnawed on. The elderly man bending over repeatedly, hunting for nuts under a hazel bush, not realizing that it's only May and the whole summer has to pass before they're ripe. And another child, yelling at a stranger from behind, quite far back—to shout an insult at him? No, to wave to the stranger when he turns around. And not to be forgotten: those people, not just a few, at the end of their strength, leaning, for example, against a tree on the roadside, not only incapable of stirring a single step from the spot but also unable to reach into their own pockets for something desperately needed, their fingers constantly curling, then flailing through the air: a key or an equally essential safety pin: "Help!" these people say to their wayward fingers, longing to recover a once cooperative body: "Help! Save me! Help me, for heaven's sake!" In reply, more derision than a reply? the rumbling in the air that was already there before, constant, not just a phenomenon of the current day, a steady background roar—radio waves?— which, however, stands out from the usual universe of sounds in the context of this cry for help. And how many no-man's-lands there continued to be, smaller and smaller but more and more numerous.

Nothing to recount from inside the bus, however, despite the trip's lasting far into the evening? Not so: I sewed a button onto my shirt cuff: a sense of snugness around my wrist, homeyness away from home. And one of the passengers scolded his mobile telephone, lying in front of him: "Stop flashing at me, you rat!" And when one of the clusters of willow and poplar catkins sailing in through the half-open window landed on the back of my hand, I could see black fly's wings stirring in the midst of the white fluff, or no: the fluff was actually part of the fly, and it was impossible to blow the "white fluff fly" (as I dubbed it) off my hand, which gave rise to the thought: "This fly will save the human race!" And the one Japanese passenger wearing a mask. And passengers named Hugger and Snuggler or Snuggler-Hugger, of whom there were quite a few. And not to be forgotten: the women in the back of the bus putting on makeup for the evening, different ones from station to station.

And yes, indeed, the abandoned church on one of the bus loops near the border between the Île-de-France and Normandy or Picardy. During a rest stop I went inside. The church was open, transformed into a bridge hall, a quiet one, with players at only one table, all women. At a second table an older woman was seated by herself, her eyes closed. No longer any trace of the church's fixtures. Yet one trace remained after all:

the Eternal Light on a side wall, electrified even back when Mass was still being celebrated, and how it reflected in the glasses propped on the bridge players' heads. And then another relic: the former confessional, now used by children playing hide-and-go-seek. And outside on the round arch over the entryway the medieval lozenge pattern, one eye connected to the next, as it were, which I imagined as a variation on the computer's @ symbol. And then look at this! thousand-year-old mason's marks, one in the form of a pyramid-shaped tree, and standing in front of the marks a jogger, as if following exercise instructions in pictograms along a fitness path. And before leaving I lit two candles there, not inside under the Eternal Light but out in the open, near the lozenges and mason's marks, one for the living and one for the dead. There I spotted my snake again; having migrated to the border, it lay curled up with another snake, soaking up the last rays of the May sun in the grass behind the former church, and it stayed there, just raising its checkered head for a moment. But another feature of this epic poem was that the shuttle-bus driver kept getting lost and had no idea how to get back on track, and each time the person who helped him out, telling him where to turn, was me. That was what the story called for.

After the ninety-ninth shuttle-bus loop, we arrived at the last stop for the evening: the destination. The inn specified in the plan: a last-stop inn if ever there was one. — How to picture it? — No particular features, except that it evoked, at least for me, the inside of a barn, though it had always, for centuries, served only as a tavern, the floor of tightly joined oak planks more like that of a dining room on an ocean liner. I sat alone for a while at one of the many tables, which were gradually filling up as evening came on, and lost myself in contemplation of those old floor planks, probably also because my head had grown heavy in the course of the day. In the many places where branches had originally grown out of the oak trunk, the earlier knots were now pits in the floor, most of them shallow, though here and there larger, deeper hollows, reminiscent of our floor back in the village, that one spruce rather than oak, where long ago we'd played our special game of marbles, not outdoors but in the house, using similar holes and hollows, and shooting clay balls we'd fashioned ourselves; and without once thinking of later games, I now felt as though that child's game had been the *summum*, again taken literally, of all our games. And I wanted a game like that for the night ahead. I "wanted"? I decreed: our decisive game. And the "we" needed no explanation.

The name of the end-of-the-line inn: "Neuf-et-Treize," Nine-and-Thirteen, and that had been its name for more than a century. Because two railway lines converged there? The dining room was almost full now, but for one table, a small one in the middle, which remained unoccupied and was supposed to stay that way; that, too, was what the story called for.

The festivities could begin. No signal or raised baton

was needed. Hanging up of coats, shifting of chairs, taking of seats combined with other movements, gestures, and actions—handshaking, brow-raising—to create a festive atmosphere, even, for some moments, solemnity. One particularly elegant handshake merely added to that effect, involving a great curved gesture from one person's forehead to the other person's hand.

Not a few of the people I'd encountered during the day had found their way there, in different guises yet the same: the singer-cum-taxi driver, the judge-cum-shepherd's pipe player. And the thought came to me, yes, the insight, that in all that time I hadn't interacted with a single bad or evil person, and not just on this day but in months, in years! Had I ever tangled with a real villain, someone fundamentally evil? Not in person, never in flesh and blood.

I saw only luminous guests around me. Even those with somber faces were bright: what a remarkable, almost (almost) unearthly brightness shone forth whenever their somberness lifted for a moment, however fleeting.

Among the couples in the hall the newcomers stood out, though I used that term not only for those who'd just met by chance, on their way to the inn, and were now trying for the first time to tell almost complete strangers who they were, where they came from, where they worked. "Newcomers" was what I also called this or that old and former couple, separated for years and now conversing again for the first time—and how the dialogue faltered, and faltered again, sustained however by mutual goodwill, and more besides. Among them the one couple from whom, later in the evening, from the man or maybe the woman, a room-filling shout was heard: "I don't want to see you ever again; get out!" and, almost in the same breath, an if possible even more ghastly howl, "We belong together, and nothing can part us, ever again, don't leave me, please, please!" and finally just a single wordless wail, which immediately gave way to singing, or an attempt at singing.

The stranger seated next to me—whom I thought of as "my dinner partner"—had placed a mobile telephone on the table and was writing a message to someone, and I couldn't help looking as it came together, letter by letter, word by word: "As I went down into the Métro, I wished that on the stairs my dress (not all women wear pants) would flutter in the wind and you would see that as you watched from above, but it was too late, and you weren't there anymore to see it" (*my translation*). Whereupon I opened my own device, and on the screen were three poems just sent to me by my friend Emmanuel, the auto-body painter, the first of which went as follows: "*Rentré à la maison comme d'habitude / Je l'aime*" ("Having returned home as usual / I love her"), and the second: "*Est-ce qu'elle de mauvaise foi? / Et alors*" ("Does she have ulterior motives? / So what?"). And here's the third: "*Il faudrait que je retombe amoureux / Ça fait oublier les points et la virgule*" ("Time to fall back in love / Then the periods and commas won't matter") (*my rough translations*).

At intervals I sat at the bar, on one of the high stools, where I had the best view of the whole restaurant. The bartender was carrying on an agitated conversation with a guest; the other man just listened in silence, and only the bartender was agitated, talking and talking. Not a few of the guests at our party kept passing through the swinging door into the kitchen, as if they belonged there as well. In my wine glass a chestnut blossom, displaying the Hogarthian line of beauty and grace. (I chewed and swallowed it.)

Back at the table, I noticed for the first time the giant television screen in a rear corner of the dining area. It was on, with the sound muted. On the screen was a group of pundits, obviously laughing a lot, baring their teeth in what seemed to be a ritual and intermittently whispering behind hands cupped over their mouths, like coaches keeping the next play secret from the opposing team. All of them had their careers as experts behind them and had become fixtures in the worldwide entertainment industry. One of the women I recognized as the perpetrator, the one who'd hurled her clueless cruelty at my mother in the grave. — Was she really the one? — I decreed that she was. She had three pairs of glasses: one perched atop her head, one hiding her eyes, and one dangling from a cord around her neck, and she kept scribbling notes with an extra-long pencil that I wished would break in half (except that, as mentioned previously, this was not a day on which wishing did any good).

And suddenly all the balls, all the marbles rolled in a direction entirely different from the one I'd intended at the beginning of this story. She, the evildoer, she and her kind didn't belong in the story, either in this one or any other. The story had no room for them. And that was my revenge. And it was revenge enough. It was and is revenge enough. Will have been revenge enough, amen. Not the sword of steel but the other one, the second sword.

She and her kind. And we here, in the dining room, we party guests: Were there others of our "kind"? No, there were no others like us, anywhere in the world. Fortunately for us? Unfortunately for us? Did we deserve to be envied, pitied, mourned? Blessèd muddle.

A sigh rang out in the dining room. — "A sigh," something "rang"? — That's how it was.

I asked my dinner partner for a pocket mirror so I could take a look at my face, an avenger's face. Yes, is that how a person looks when he's just succeeded in carrying out the revenge he's been dreaming of for a long time? From the mirror I gazed out at myself, looking merry, merry as I'd hardly ever experienced myself, with pure levity in the corners of my eyes. "Bridegroom! Bridegroom!" I heard a blackbird, past its bedtime, calling, for my sake, in the words of a German children's song, or was it a nightingale? And whatever it was, the bird wasn't singing; it was shouting. It was bawling. And as an accompaniment the drumming of Faulkner's wild palms.

Material for another story: how I groped my way home in the dark, arriving in the gray of dawn at my garden gate without my key and, as I recall, on all fours, while from the woods on the Eternal Hill came the first pops of a hunter's rifle. But I'll leave that story for someone else to tell.

—April–May 2019
Île-de-France/Picardy

MY DAY
IN THE
OTHER
LAND

A TALE
OF
DEMONS

ἐγὼ δὲ ἴδιος ἐν κοινῷ σταλείς

I, the idiot [Gk. = a private person], setting sail on

my own course for the common good

—Pindar, *Olympian XIII*, line 49

1

In my life there's a story that I've never told a soul. And now that I'm putting it out into the world, very late in the day, I must mention that neither the words nor the images I'm about to share at the beginning originate with me, though I myself am the main character and the only active figure. This story: I lived its first part in flesh and blood, more viscerally than almost all the other stories in my life. But my knowledge of it comes entirely from hearsay—from the accounts of others: my family, and, more intensely and extensively, third parties, the people of my village, if not, more influentially today, total strangers from surrounding towns and far beyond. It's not simply that I have no recollection of that time, not a trace in my memory, not the "faintest inkling"; at the time in question, as I heard later, some people thought I was in an unconscious state, others that I was out of my mind. "Unconscious" was the family version, harking back to tales of quite a few of our ancestors who had apparently been given to a kind of sleepwalking—with the wrinkle in my case that it also took place by day. But in the eyes of all those not in the family, I was "out of my mind."

Outside of our four walls it was considered a fact that I was possessed, possessed by not just one but by several, many, even innumerable demons. "Outside of our four walls": that included the information, imparted to me later, that I'd eventually broken out of our property and—believe it or not—pitched my tent, a very small one, on the outskirts of the village, in a graveyard, not the current one but the "old one," the former one, where most of the graves from the two previous centuries were abandoned or overgrown.

I was also told that while I was in the grip of madness my work as a fruit farmer—my main occupation from early on—was handled by my only sister. When I mentioned "the family" earlier, I was actually referring only to my sister; my father and mother were long gone, and in the house and the surrounding area the two of us were the only ones left; and long before my sleepwalking, or taking leave of my senses, my sister had been lending me a hand in the many, diversified orchards around what had been our parental home. She was the one who would visit me, I learned, if not daily at least once or twice a week, in my remote corner of the old cemetery to provide me with what was most needful. Needful? According to my sister, during my life as a sleepwalker I needed hardly anything other than our own apples, Jonathans, Boskoops, Ontarios, and above all Gravensteins—planted before the war by our father—and our homemade bread, which had beechnuts and hazelnuts baked in, my favorite food since childhood but, during the time in question, said to appeal to me even more.

Here a memory of my own at last: back when I, the fruit farmer, was more or less clear in the head and, if I may say so, thanks to my occupation, the epitome of presence of mind, now and then there was something distinctly odd, uncanny, even sinister about me. Certain children had a special ability to sniff that out, even at a distance. Not a few of them, upon catching sight of me, would take off running in the opposite direction, but after a few steps would stop and stare at me over their shoulders, the way foxes do, whereupon I would be the one giving them a wide berth so as not to scare them.

Yet there were also people of my own age, and not them alone but even more often older ones, especially the very old, from whom I would hear from time to time that they weren't sure "where they stood" with the fruit farmer. "Something's not right about you, starting with your cowlick!" In the village certain expressions came into currency, such as "moody as a fruit farmer" or "with a fruit farmer's evil eye," or "more fruit-farmer-ish than a fruit farmer" or "His Highness the fruit farmer," or also, in a friendlier vein, "as unworldly and skittish as a fruit farmer."

At the time my sister speculated that those negative

opinions of me—which sprang up now and then, only
to die down the next day—stemmed from the fact that
as a young man, shortly after graduating from horticul-
ture school, I'd written a book, actually no more than a
pamphlet, on fruit-tree cultivation, "The Three Meth-
ods for Raising Trees on Espaliers," but rumored to be
a book, something unfamiliar in our region, considered
pretentious, if not an assertion of power, and a fraud-
ulent power at that, a falsified power. "The power-mad
fruit farmer!"

The year, or years, during which I was possessed
apparently solidified the others' view of me as plainly
and hopelessly evil, the very spawn of evil, an incurably
evil being. According to my dear, good sister, that verdict seemed justified every time I ventured out of "my"
graveyard and became "impossible to miss" around
town. Where previously some of my quirks had given
people reason to smile, there was no more of that now.

As soon as I set foot on the village's main street, so
I heard, people not only steered clear of me but fled
to the safety of their houses. "You frightened them,
spread fear. It had nothing to do with the way you were
dressed; somehow you always managed to emerge from
your hiding place looking clean and decent, positively
elegant. Nor did it result from anything you did; no one
ever saw you acting improperly, and you passed through
the village without making any rude gestures, not even
pointing. The fear came from your words, from what the
others, the whole community, couldn't help hearing.

No, not that either. You didn't shout, let alone bellow, howl, or gnash your teeth. You spoke almost softly, in what might be called an indoor voice, seemingly to yourself, yet every word you murmured became audible, as if amplified by loudspeakers, from one end of the village to another."

All my utterances, so I was told, consisted of insults and abuse, and I kept coming up with new expressions, previously unheard-of, and then even more unheard-of. It was impossible to tell whom I was abusing and insulting. More often than at several people or a group I aimed my words at individuals, and now and then, my sister said, it was myself I seemed to be calling "incorrigible!" "pathetic!" "spawn of hell!" "worthless!" "troublemaker!" "rotten to the core!" And a sign that I was the intended target of these insults: only when I was spewing them in my community-spanning harangue did my voice get somewhat louder, and once or twice during my crazed years I actually escalated to "shouts, no, the briefest of shrieks."

At the time, my sister had the impression, if only for fleeting moments, that I was also playing a game. Or thus: that without my intending it or playing along, a game was being played inside me, a strange one; and all it would take was the presence of other players, others ready to play, not just one or two, not just a few but many! for the fear, the near-horror that I caused, to dissolve into thin air, into play-air, and what a dance that would be!

But if my behavior was meant to be an invitation to come and play, not once and not anywhere did others do me the favor of spontaneously joining in. Instead they took to their heels whenever yours truly showed his face, and that went on for years. It seemed clear: the near-terror I inspired in my fellow humans with my ceaseless asides would someday turn into actual terror, into a slaughter, a running amok, such as the area, the country, yes, the world, had never witnessed. Yet how weary I'd grown in the course of spouting endless curses and threats as I passed the old and the new, more and more identical houses in this region of which I'd once been so fond. And how the impression grew that it wasn't I who needed them but rather they who needed me, this seemingly dangerous possessed being, for the fear I inspired, one of their most unmistakable proofs of being alive. "Weary and needy, needy and weary": a line from a song?

In this connection I'm reminded of the day when, as I was zigzagging through the village, I suddenly fell silent, just moving my lips soundlessly, and sank onto the high stone doorstep of one of the last of the old houses, and sat there and sat until long after the first stars had come out, invisible, as I recall, not seen by anyone; or was I? But not as a scary ghost, and certainly not as a figure of menace.

Now, decades later, as I sit at my desk in the shed next to my house, I can feel myself on that granite doorstep, and I know that feeling neither from my sister's tales nor from the tales of others. I know it from deep inside me, from there alone. And I owe that certainty to the fact that I've finally begun to write this story down; that I've summoned the appropriate words; that a rhythm suitable for accentuating the words has presented itself, at least for now—or seems to have presented itself at any rate. This writing has unexpectedly awakened me and shown me what I was like back then as a doorstep-sitter: wide awake in my weariness, without a trace of sleepwalking or demonic possession. That is and remains, here and now, the only image I have of myself from that period. And in truth it's not an image; my memory holds nothing visual, neither the doorstep nor myself, only the sensation of sitting, sitting there, as wide awake as can be and in complete possession of my mind, entirely rational, which means entirely at peace as well.

The result—as I now imagine, or picture it—was that perhaps the very next day, or maybe already that night, the mania and raving burst out of me all the more furiously. Whatever the case, according to my sister's accounts and reports, which this time matched those of others, this final period of my derangement, before the so-called demons released me, "as if by a miracle," was—especially when it came to what my world and the world at large, including heaven and earth, had to put up with from me as a person (or monster)—characterized by the most violent and at the same time most ludicrous utterances, hardly to be taken seriously anymore.

Except when I was in my decommissioned graveyard, far from civilization, I raged against all of Creation, and no longer confined my tirades to my village and the neighboring villages, but aimed them at the whole land, small though it was; and eventually I stopped covering my mouth with my hand and instead yelled bloody murder at the top of my lungs, "without getting hoarse" (as this person or that informed me later, in those very words).

Nothing about the Creation was to my liking. Nothing about it was acceptable to me. The smallest detail—and its opposite!—rubbed me the wrong way, I was told. "Down with the Creation!" I would proclaim at the end of each stanza, as it were, the coda to yet another denunciation of some heaven-and-earth phenomenon, as harmless as it was innocent.

I'd blasted one passerby because his arms swung wide as he walked, and the next one because his arms remained stiffly at his side. I'd barked, "Shut up!" at the blackbirds trilling in the treetops. A high forehead was too high for me, and one less high too low. When a person spoke in a bass voice, he was disturbing the peace, and likewise a tenor voice was a sheer insult. "Away with all the broad shoulders, and the same with all the narrow ones. Long legs as ridiculous as short ones. How ugly you are with your thin lips, and you, with the thick ones, too, in a different way. And how come you're either ridiculously quiet or howl like wolves? That man or woman with the receding chin is as annoying as the one with a chin like a beak, the hooked noses as revolting as the pug noses, all the small breasts as indecent as the huge ones, the blonde as ancient looking as the person with snow-white hair. Ugly, ugly: it should be prohibited. And ugliest of all those of you who have no distinguishing features, you, the overwhelming majority who take up most of the room on earth, you with normal gaits, normal foreheads, normal noses, normal lips, normal jaws, normal shoulders, and, more and more, most of you newborns, looking like little copies of your normal mothers and fathers, which makes it disgustingly possible to predict how you'll look thirty, forty, fifty years from now—except that, heaven help us, unlike those before your time, hardly any of you newborns will ever have the faces of elderly men and women.

"And the eternal sameness just as dispiriting as all the things that never stop changing. The apple blossoms with five, or at most six, petals, the way they've always been. The pear blossoms stinking like carrion as always. And you, quince blossoms, always the purest of white: When will you ever change color, or at least show the tiniest vein of red? Clover, stiffen your stem so you can stand up straight under the weight of a bumblebee! And all the elongated horse skulls in the landscape. And all the unchanging butterfly flight paths. And the swirling of leaves as they fall, which can be calculated according to the strength or absence of wind. And the eternal swooping of the swallows. And the glowing of the fireflies. And the heavy breathing of the mating hedgehogs. And away with you, swan necks, wasp waists, lion manes, goat leaps!

"On the one hand the visible so disturbingly and outrageously visible; the obvious so nerve- and soul-deadeningly obvious. And on the other hand the invisible, and it's not just the blackbird in the tree, the cricket in the grass, the lark high in the sky that's maddeningly invisible, from A to Z invisible, hideously and hatefully invisible. Hateful blue of the sky. Down with the Creation!"

Such were the rants that I spat out in the last phase of my demonic possession as I roved back and forth across the land. (Was the only thing missing my foaming at the mouth? No one mentioned that. Other than occasional loud outbursts, I reportedly behaved decently, directing my tirades not at anyone personally but rather past everyone into thin air, addressing the land in general, also often speaking behind me, over my shoulder.)

That was how it went during the day, and toward evening I'd return on foot or be driven, and not only by my sister, to my campsite in the old graveyard; the land, as already mentioned, was small, no more than a few valleys separated by brooks and ponds, which made returning for the night possible.

Even now I still feel the need once a day to be out in public, not in the sense of wanting to show myself or put in an appearance, but of finding a space that allows me to get out and away from the private sphere: the public as an arena without which a day doesn't qualify as a proper day; public space as a sort of fountain of youth.

During that time, once I came back to my spot in the remote corner, home from the speaking crusades that took me hither and yon, I inevitably underwent a transformation. I still had no consciousness of myself, remaining oblivious, as during the day, to my actions and what issued from my mouth, or at least I have no memory of such things. But according to others, I no sooner set foot in the former burial ground, hardly recognizable as such anymore, than I became the epitome of gentleness. If I did open my mouth and make myself heard—far and wide!—the sounds that rang out were the complete opposite of the cascades of swearing and cursing heard earlier. Rang out? Yes, rang out, and in a way that, without exaggeration—or only a slight one—penetrated the most distant dwellings in the valleys of our land.

As people described it, I constantly alternated between speaking and singing. And my speaking didn't happen in our native tongue, but also, no matter how carefully articulated each word was, not in any other living language; even the region's one and only world-famous linguistics expert couldn't assign my totally alien idiom to any other, let alone name it. At any rate, not one of my words was comprehensible. And yet it was as clear as day to those with ears to hear that in this unknown language, with its mysterious syntax and undecodable grammar, I was expressing reassurances impossible to formulate effectively in any known local language, not to mention any of the so-called world languages.

The odd part was that now and then someone, drawn by the sound of my voice—usually a child from the surrounding area rebelling at having to go to bed so early in summertime—would sneak up on me and discover that instead of speaking into thin air I was always addressing some living being, a single animal or a pair, or several. Butterflies? Birds? Grasshoppers? Dragonflies? Snails? Transformed in the evening from a dangerous madman into a harmless idiot, I was talking to muskrats, owls, bats, wildcats, martens, lynx, turtles, lizards, snakes. And it seemed as if some of these animals, when they heard my voice, would actually pause for a moment in the middle of devouring, hunting, or flying in search of prey (except the bats).

My singing, when it issued forth from my corner of the steppe, with its grasses, brush, and tumbledown stone walls, was decidedly quiet, without the ringing and resonance of what I articulated in the unknown language: singing pure and simple, with not a single word. Only a few people heard it, but they reported later that it had created something like an echo. But from where? — "From every nook and cranny"; "an eventide sound"; "a song for eventide."

One of those few was my sister, and at first she didn't want to believe that I was the singer. She'd never heard her brother sing that way. "In the past, before your twilight period, if you sang, you deliberately sang off-key, as off-key as you could! And then what a contrast those few times! You never sang again, either that way or intentionally off-key! And how you sang, demon, almost inaudibly, but with such glowing eyes, listening to the echo as if you couldn't believe your singing yourself, a demon through and through!"

After that, so I was told, came a brief period, before everything abruptly dissolved into thin air like a mirage, during which I achieved the status of an authority for some people, or just a few, in the area and the land; and occasionally it was almost possible to speak of a "throng" seeking me out in the back of the graveyard, now reverted to savanna.

During that final episode in my seeming madness, or, as I'm going to call it, now that I'm writing about it, my "self-transcendence," I functioned for this person or that as a kind of oracle. My oracular pronouncements, however, pertained to neither a future nor a past, nor did they take the form of riddles. I would simply tell the person to his face what was up with him and how it looked for him, not just now, in the moment, but from the very beginning.

My pronouncements were issued unceremoniously, and at a time when they were no longer, or not yet, expected, catching the recipients off guard and unsuspecting. Without exception they consisted of one short statement, an arrow that unfailingly hit the target. And

the person seeking enlightenment felt more than merely
pinned: he understood that I, the idiot with the gentle
gaze, had recognized him once and for all, for better and
worse. In such situations my face displayed none of the
absent quality it usually wore in my abode on the steppe:
during the brief, sudden moment when my verdict was
pronounced, my face glowed with a presence of mind
that suggested the same thing to all the oracle-seeking
pilgrims: I was performing something like an official
duty, one that was self-evident and no big deal.

This authority of mine had hardly anything to do
with reading the oracle seekers' physiognomies and
tones of voice. — Was it perhaps what's called "eidetic
vision": perception of essences? — "Essences" may be
right, but not "vision," for don't vision and visualiz-
ing imply something lasting and consistent over a period of time? Here, however, in the case of the mentally
disturbed individual (i.e., me in those days), whose
spontaneous utterance of truth hit the bull's-eye every
time, no vision or visualization had taken place before-
hand; each pronouncement shot out of me with a jolt,
for which one of my visitors in those days, an expert
in the rarest, understudied, and, to this day, still understudied psychic aberrations, later came up with a
technical term: "the demonic jolt." That label, however,
in the fraction of a second when my arrow hit him almost, or exactly, simultaneously with the pertinent vol-
ley of words—"You're a born traitor" or something of
the sort—apparently didn't protect him from losing his

professional cool, though for a mere fraction of another second.

Besides, the chapter on those demonic jolts, which were not just peaceable but furthermore, what's the expression? "community-enhancing," was also fleeting and soon a thing of the past, like that speaking in tongues of mine, which harrowed or scoured the land in a nonexistent language, or my singing from the throat of a nameless little angel. Mute, after falling silent and swallowing my tongue, I'm described as either cowering in my quasi-desertlike refuge during the long summer evenings and the nights filled with cricket-chirping, or sitting enthroned: "On your knees, invisible subjects!"

All the greater was the tumult that characterized my final days of public appearances in those parts. Incidentally, by then I was by no means the only one causing a commotion around the houses, on the streets, and at the markets, merely playing at being possessed according to some, actually possessed according to others. As the years went by, new demoniacs had turned up from God knows where, both older and younger, and almost as many women as men; to date only a child was lacking.

All of us were tolerated. It was as if each had a district of his own (except for me, for whom that area had no borders). Not one of the growing number of town-and-country criers ever ran into another, and if one did, he had neither eyes nor—heaven forbid—ears for the other. And it was as if each of us—and we weren't really that many—all out of our minds without hope of return, were an institution, part of the region's profile, and also serving the public interest.

Could that be true? That we who'd gone irrevocably off our rockers served the public interest? Yes, in the sense that, without being aware of it (how would we have been?), we held up a mirror to the rest of the population. A mirror showing what? A mirror showing the danger lurking inside them: "That's how I secretly am myself, and it's possible that tomorrow morning, or as soon as this evening, from one moment to the next all of it could come pouring out of me in screams, and I might go on screaming, screeching, and raving without end." But isn't it true that at most a small minority is at risk of this, by no means the whole population? — On the contrary: it's the whole population, all of it! — And what interest did they have in being mirrored by us, the possessed? — That mirroring could, if not heal people, at least pull them up short for a moment, just as objects keep one in line, preserving form and forms, especially out here with all the others watching, and, as specifically mentioned, in the public interest!

On my very last day as the self-appointed king of the countrywide demonship, in which each had his own district, a particular variant manifested itself in the characteristic mirroring. I'd roamed several Greek or American miles and Russian versts from my sleeping place in the graveyard, and as usual was traversing the land's public areas, when, for a change, no one from the general population showed any interest in me. Maybe that resulted, among other things, from the fact that I didn't open my mouth the entire time, which meant all day, and also refrained from making my usual gestures. I didn't lift a finger, move a lip, or raise an eyebrow. I couldn't even be caught blinking. — Who observed that? And who described it? — My sister, who at the time was very worried about me and secretly followed me every morning; she thought I might be even less in my right mind than before, if possible.

And this is the variation: those who did notice me on my daylong back-and-forth were the others, "my people," from district to district. And at the sight of their chief madman, their hue and cry—"instead of from the depths of their souls, from a bottomless absence of soul," as my sister put it—didn't merely die in their throats; I was told they turned away and covered their faces with their hands, all in the same rhythm. And then my fellow demons took to their heels as only demons can? Not at all: these demons went into hiding, so the story goes, or at least looked around for a place to hide. These demons were ashamed, and not of me but of themselves, or maybe thus: at the spectacle of my craziness they felt ashamed of their own fake craziness, their imitation of demonic possession. Demons and shame! And after that most of them disappeared, never to be seen again. "And what's more," commented my sister, an expert in spite of herself, "no real demon, once he's found his proper place, will let himself be chased away; he's unchaseable. But those others . . ."

My sister's concern at this point was no longer that I was a danger to others but that I was a danger to myself. Even as a child I'd announced, especially to my mother, that someday I was going to bash myself headfirst into the cliff behind our house, throw myself into the manure pit, do a somersault from the top of the cherry tree in the village square, and I'd uttered these threats with such conviction that my mother wasn't the only one who had to take them seriously.

Let me add here, going beyond my sister's anxiety about me, a fragmentary personal memory from those last hours when I was possessed: an intuition that it wouldn't be myself I'd harm but the local children, who, in the meantime, having begun by imitating me, had become my followers, in flesh and blood, uttering cries of rage and disgust, and recoiling from the world, if not from the universe like me. It was them, the children, I would kill, one and all! A second slaughter of the innocent was in the offing! Help!

In the end I was reduced, day in, day out, to screams. But it was a screaming that remained bottled up, a screaming with lips closed, voiceless, without vowels, only consonants: "k!," "n!," "p!," "s!," and so forth. Instead of crying out I cried in, and incessantly, without pause. And no one there who heard me, let alone listened to me. No one who needed me. My sister probably acted as if she did. But it was a fake act, and only made things worse.

2

On the day in question my sister—and she alone—saw me cry as I'd never cried even in childhood. (And in fact it was during my period of demonic possession that for the first and only time she experienced me crying.) I cried, silently, for help; that I bared my teeth was part of that crying for help, and the sight of my whole body shaking and shuddering eventually revealed to my sister what I, incapable of making a sound, wanted to cry out of my system.

The cries for help took the form of denunciations and curses, all aimed at myself. "If I could just be struck by lightning. If only someone would pull a knife on me and stab me in the heart. If only that rural bus would skid off the road and flatten me. If only the old oak would fall on my head. Into the hopper of the garbage truck with me, to be compacted. Into the cage with the hungry lion. Or at least let a flock of pigeons fly over and shit on me from head to foot!"

It came to pass that my sister blocked my way, and furthermore that I took a step toward her, and, standing a hand's breadth from her face, spoke insistently to her in a soft but distinct voice from deep inside me, and, what's more, spoke in complete, largely rational sentences (though at the same time it wasn't clear, as in the preceding months and years of madness, whether I recognized her): "Hello, how goes it? What's terrible isn't the darkness but rather the light, inside me and all around me. How evil this light is. I'm imprisoned in it. Lightbound all around and in the smallest interstices of my soul. Ah, what chambers once occupied this space, chamber after chamber with the most delicate partial shade and the most inviting, gleaming dusk. Clandestine dwellings and refuges, opening their doors as needed and also without any need, more and more of them, one and all softly glowing without any supplemental light, let alone extraneous light—extraneous light upon extraneous light—in which *it* could happen, would soon be revealed—it! And in the meantime: woe, the light cancer eating away at my soul: overhead lighting, underlighting, frontal lighting, backlighting, sidelighting, central lighting, exterior lighting, indoor lighting, all at once, inescapable, neither al-Rahîm nor al-Rahmân, not the merciful one or merciful thing, to say nothing of the all-merciful: merciless. Woe and again woe. Helpless me, beyond help!"

And my eyes wide during this tirade, and if possible

wider still with every sentence, incapable of closing, and not only since this particular morning.

And again it came to pass or turned out that my sister and I were standing on the bank of a lake, the only one in our land, with the other land on the opposite shore. A few men were hauling a fishing boat out of the water, and remained standing for a while, forming a half circle. But it wasn't that which I saw and which, in an instant! after years of near-unconsciousness restored me to consciousness.

What roused me and let me return to my former self were the eyes of the man in the middle of the half circle. Although at some distance from me and my sister, and furthermore with the light behind the man intensified by the lake's surface, the pair of pupils was very close to me—any closer would have been impossible—and crisply defined, though without an identifiable color. And I felt, no, I knew these eyes were looking at me as I'd never been looked at before by a human being. It wasn't just a looking-at but beyond that, no, added to that! an observing, purely companionable, selflessly empathetic, friendly. It didn't want to be seen. And was seen nonetheless. And how! My heart stood still, and resumed beating a moment later, stronger than ever.

There he was at long last, the Good Observer I'd been so sorely in need of during my spell of madness. And truly "in no time" I was rid of the demon; the demons had fled. No trace of a stench either. It was as if they'd dissolved into thin air. (And now, as I'm writing this story down, an actual/real puff of scent reaches my nostrils, a blend of rare perfume, not bad at all, of which I hope everyone reading this will catch a whiff.)

What did "Good Observer" signify? It signified, for example, the following: his observing was simultaneously a form of looking and listening—keeping an ear cocked even when there was nothing to hear. And the Good Observer expected neither praise nor a reward for his observing, in that respect entirely different from so many of the current professional observers, including the organized ones; and above all he practiced his observing neither for profit nor power!—or at least not any commercial or institutional form of power.

Back in life; returned to the world, the beloved planet, Mother Earth. First a hug for my sister—"So there you are!"—and slobbering all over her face while at the same time pulling her hair, as in the old days, everything at once, then falling to my knees, boom! without taking into account that along with the years of madness my youth had flown. Youth or not: at any rate, as I knelt there I yawned as only newborns yawn.

My genuflection must almost have looked as though it were intended for the one whose Good-Observer gaze had freed me from my evil spell, for in the meantime he'd left the circle of lake fishermen and made his way toward me. But I'd fallen to my knees involuntarily, almost in spite of myself, and accordingly I jumped up before the stranger reached me.

To him I was no stranger, at any rate. Why else would he have placed his hand on my shoulder with such tender casualness—despite, or thanks to, which I still feel that hand on me today—and greeted me, saying, "There you are, my friend!" No one had ever called me his friend that way. And my sister told me then and there that during her visits to me on the steppe, she'd run into him time and again, and one fine day she'd even come upon him across from me, though "at an appropriate distance," among the nearly sunken grave mounds, reading a book, and occasionally looking up and in my direction, and then at her. "Yes, and eventually he became my sweetheart, and that he's remained. Just so you know, brother of mine."

Meanwhile the fishermen from the lakeshore had all drawn closer, and now they formed their semicircle around me, my sister, and her *ami*; and when I saw all of us standing there together, my eyes fresher than ever before, it came to me that this was the best possible and loveliest of communities, and under a summer-morning sky, too, and with the roar of the lake's ocean-high waves, and I said, or heard myself stammering, "Oh, let me stay with all of you forever, or at least for this one day."

But then came the response: at first only from my "Good Observer," but then from my "dear sister," chiming in, and finally from the "chorus of lake fishermen": "No, you don't belong here with us, friend. You have no business here. Away with you. And there's not a moment to lose; hop to it! Get yourself to the land across the lake, neighbor. And there you'll tell your story, and share with the people in the Decapolis, the former Land of Ten Cities, what happened to you, understood? One stadion, or about a hundred ninety meters from here, deep in the rushes, you'll find a boat with a one-handed rudder and an outboard motor and everything you'll need for the other land, and that will get you over the lake. Away with you, and fare-thee-well, friend—brother—neighbor!"

So now, freed of my demons, I made my way across to the other land, though not until after a protracted leave-taking. The boat was small, meant for one occupant, light as aluminum but also stable, and besides, once one got past the belt of rushes, the lake had almost no waves at first, as smooth as a pond, and indeed it resembled a large pond, even though very long ago the common folks' term for it had been "sea," "our sea." The shore of the other land could be seen as soon as I set out.

In the boat I found a change of clothes, with provisions in the pockets. Once in these clothes, I felt something had been accomplished, or cleared out of the way.

I rowed effortlessly, left, right, as if in a canoe, which I pictured as painted in Indian colors. From the instant I set out until I tied up across the lake, I had no need to start the motor, and the thought didn't cross my mind. For moments at a time I didn't even have to dip the oars: as if I were being propelled along. Or as if the waves now forming without the slightest breeze were pushing the boat toward the yonder shore (you read that right: "yonder"). And as a musical accompaniment the completely silent flickering and fluttering on the keyboard of the waves.

When I first climbed into the boat, a leech, barely the length of my little finger, was lying in a rain puddle in the bottom of the boat, seemingly waiting for me, so I placed it on the back of one of my calves, but it fell off without managing to get its teeth into me, let alone fill up on my blood, and kept falling off, again and again, either spurning me or sparing me, so I abandoned it among the bulrushes, on an ear that almost matched its color.

"If I ever get to return," I told the leech, "you mustn't spurn my blood. May you find it tasty—the blood of the Good Observer's envoy."

The stillness after that on the pond, or lake, became transformed during the time I granted myself for the crossing—o the joy, the peace, of having time!—into what Goethe called oceanic stillness, and memories of my school days came flooding back in association with the ancient Greek word for such stillness: "*galênê* (γαλήνη)."

The shore of the other land had no belt of rushes, and in contrast to ours had steep cliffs. But from the top of the cliffs extended what appeared at first to be a plain like ours, without hills, which, as a result of the climb involved in reaching it, created the impression, if only briefly, of a highland, that of the former Decapolis, the ten-settlement highland, long since vanished but for a few traces and replaced by a single, more or less thickly settled polis or community.

But enough geography now; back to me. My story is the important thing: how I spent the first day after my salvation, that one above all, and then at least an intimation of what followed: the weeks, months, years.

Stepping out of the boat and setting foot on the shore of the other land, I found I'd gone blind. Or to put it another way: I could see, but not with my eyes. My eyes suddenly left me in the lurch, replaced by—"Did you see that? Come on, open wide!"—some other form of perception, located in my shoulders, fingertips, soles. The sense of touch? no: for instead of groping my way onto land and up the cliff, I forged ahead and climbed, seemingly blind, without hesitation, without a single tentative step, my hand grasping the right hold on the rock every time, my head and shoulders drawn back to avoid every sharp edge. And it was almost disappointing, once I reached the rim of the Decapolis plateau, to regain my usual ability to see, the "light of my eyes." Ah, to have that blindness prolonged, ye powers! But no.

Overcome by a kind of indignation, I yanked off my glasses, hoping to not see clearly, to be spared distinct outlines! The first and only feature I could initially make out in the other land was partially hidden by the blurry leaves of unidentified trees—foliage the only thing I recognized—a gabled house. And the gable, jutting out of its isosceles triangle, greeted me as gables had greeted me for as long as I could recall, except during my time of terror. And as if involuntarily I was already putting on my seeing-clearly glasses. Yes, the gable greeted me and welcomed me, and how. And in spite of that, from then on I made it my practice from time to time during the rest of that day to find my way in that land without assistive devices, imposing more and more new rules on myself, or actually just rules of the game. But why "just"? Look! Do you see that blank window in the gable—it just opened. — Nonsense! It's been open for quite a while. — But the circle of rays on the roof; didn't it come from the TV dish? — So what? The rays radiate.

Rules, whether these or others. I was aware that this one day in the other land, my first with unfettered heart and calm senses, would be dangerous. I'd be tested to the maximum. Tested by whom? Just tested, without a who or what.

The houses that came after the first one, each separated by a great distance from its neighbor, didn't have gables. Although a smooth paved road led to the interior of the land, at first I didn't encounter a single person and heard no human voices, not even from a radio or television (yet the roofs sported a welter of antennas). The only sound of civilization I heard far and wide came through the strikingly numerous gratings in the pavement, from the sewers, a ceaseless, steady roaring and rushing.

The following "rules": don't stop before evening if you can help it; maintain the pace you set once you reached the top of the cliff; stick to the highways, paved with tar or asphalt for cars; steer clear of hiking trails; don't consult any maps, let alone trail guides; do your best to avoid nature, especially forests and trees, or view them only as a backdrop or distant horizon; keep to the shoulder of the main arteries, beneath the open sky.

Likewise I decided that all day long my eyes should avoid fixating on particulars. No details! Likewise I should refrain from collecting, from picking up objects and pocketing them. And no sideways glances! Keep my eyes aimed straight ahead, or down at my moving feet, or behind me at others' feet and the bare pavement, or, as a onetime exception (not more), skyward (what was allowed, however, was seeing, registering things involuntarily, out of the corner of my eye). Every time I violated the rules, however slightly, the game constantly playing out deep inside me required that I retrace my steps to a field I'd already passed or suffer this consequence: as a penalty my new, demon-free life would be cut short by a week, if not a month. Just one quick, hardly intentional sideways glance at a half-overgrown path leading from the road into a thicket—once almost irresistible to me—and another portion of my life would be gambled away; the same if I glanced to one side at a cricket sitting by its hole in the ground.

Not covered by rules like these, however, was the anonymity of so much of what I happened upon as I made my way through the other land. Nameless birds sang. Nameless flowers bloomed. A nameless bug let me carry it on my hand until early dusk. And this namelessness brought relief; was part of my liberation; enhanced further my joy at being rid of the last few years, a nameless, vibrating joy that signified living for the first time, being alive. Away with you, names, and likewise away with "elderberry," "Shetland pony," "cedars of Lebanon," as well as "Aaron's staff," "paradise apple," "Jesus pear," "passion fruit"! The only name for something in nature for which I made allowances during my day in the other land was "stinging nettle": having been roused from unconsciousness, as an expression of my sudden, fresh joy in being alive I'd plunged my hand into a nettle on the shore, and the burning sensation kept me company for the rest of the day.

Another thing not dictated by a rule was that I ate nothing until evening. The lake water I'd drunk in the morning had refreshed me, and I needed nothing else; no temptation to reach out even once to pluck some of the innumerable blackberries along the road, already ripe. And besides, when I passed trucks at midday parked by the road, with the workmen, or whatever they were, often in pairs, having their lunch in the cab, I felt as though I were eating with them, at their invitation. Yes, that made me hungry; I felt hunger. But it was a revitalizing hunger.

It was a workday on which I was making my way through that unfamiliar land, or land that had become unfamiliar, yet wherever I looked I had the sensation of its being a holiday. Ah, what an odd holiday, not noted in any calendar on the five (or however many) continents, and furthermore a new holiday on each stretch of road, and all the holidays different from one another.

On the first stretch of road, still devoid of people, the holiday became the "Day of the Disappeared." I finally recalled stories I'd heard from my sister about quite a few of our ancestors who'd disappeared, either in our own land or elsewhere, without a word, and never to be seen again. "We, the tribe of the disappeared." And that included for me, the younger sibling, my parents, who'd left little or no impression on me. But now, in the continuing absence of other people on the road, I caught sight of them for an instant (see the corner of my eye)—my mother and father crossing the road as airy outlines, along with other missing persons, the latter without outlines.

And on the next stretch through the other land, or the stretch after that, or whichever, I celebrated the "Feast of My Unborn Children." This road, at any rate, was already more or less populated, and the first human being I'd encountered earlier had been a child, a little fellow just taking his first steps, energetically pushing away the hands eager to help him. This child sought to meet my eyes, and I cooperated, meeting his gaze, also a new experience for me on this "first day." And that turned into a festivity, in fact the feast of unborn children, when I refused to let the two or three children who now sought my gaze turn away, disappointed for life. I'd observed that most of the children whose paths I crossed on stretch after stretch of road made no attempt to meet any adult's eyes, not mine and not anyone else's. But what an image resulted from that first child, the smallest one, who'd begun with me and with whom I'd begun: the way he'd responded to my answering gaze by taking a few steps backward, as if for my sake, though seemingly so unsteady on his little legs, as if walking backward were the most natural thing in the world for little children taking their first steps. And part of that image was his eyes, which made the expression "child's play" acquire a whole different meaning.

As I played through the possible meanings of that expression in my mind, I was also playing for time as I made my way along the road, pausing to take in the play of shadows on the ground as I passed under trees brushed now and then by a playful breeze until, emerging into the open, I looked up and registered the spectacle of sunlight forming a halo around the edges of the fluffy clouds in the azure sky above. I took that halo as a blessing.

Another image: the waves of grass far off on the rim of the horizon: if I'd been closer to them, I'd never have felt so close to them. And against the backdrop of the distant forest with its towering crowns, the sky looked like blue shirts hung out to dry, one blue shirt after the other: those shirts struck a chord with me now. As far as I could tell, this was my first time in this land. But how did it happen that I exclaimed at one point, "Here I am again!" And after that, "Here we are again, yes, we are!"

Illusion and yet more illusion. So what? In one way or another I accepted blessings and blessedness as real on that first day of my freedom, no matter what happened afterward. I was experiencing them, after all. At the outset I'd shaken the dust from my feet, and not only in a figurative sense, till the dust rose almost to my eyebrows, and after that nothing rubbed me the wrong way, and that persisted beyond this one day.

True: most of the people in this other land didn't merely overlook me; to them I was nonexistent. Accordingly, they bumped into me without meaning to (especially the runners, who were everywhere), elbowed me aside, trod on my heels with no regard for my excellent old shoes, but that was all right by me. Or rather, neither all right nor not all right. Those people—never just one, usually groups, smaller as well as larger ones—didn't count, as indeed for me it was a day without likes or dislikes, also free of patience or impatience. All my perhaps innate impatience—the "mother of my demons"? "impatience the original demon"?—was no longer in play, and along with it patience, that helper in time of need. I no longer had any need of patience. And those who overlooked me or even deliberately ignored me were fine as far as I was concerned. They gave me something against which to measure myself.

There were others in that land to whom my presence

proved beneficial, not that I was anything like a benefactor; it happened simply as a result of my showing myself and being the way I was (not "reinventing" myself but discovering myself). I just did one person or another good, and that was no illusion. And on one stretch of road after another it was always single individuals in whom I inadvertently and in passing discovered allies, which they in turn discovered in me. Strange alliances.

It didn't occur to me, despite the instructions my Good Observer had given, to describe to people in the former Decapolis how things had stood with me before now and what had happened that morning on the lakeshore. I walked along in silence, saying nothing till evening. And yet something about me must have conveyed an impression of what I'd been through and projected it into the land, a certain something that long after sunset the woman who would later be my wife expressed when she said, "You seem to come from afar, sir."

Every individual stranger I met along the road exchanged a greeting with me. It consisted of our raising our heads and smiling, and the smile was the greeting, spreading across the whole face, entirely different from the proverbial last laugh. It was an exception when the greetings took place simultaneously, and likewise an exception when I was the first to greet and draw the greeting out of the other—I always knew in advance that it would come, and was less surprised than pleased, and with all my heart, and also knew in advance who wouldn't respond to a greeting, which of the passersby was "ungreetable," and not just to me, so I had no need to meet the other person's eyes.

Usually it was the other person, the stranger, who greeted me first, with seemingly casual familiarity, as if I were a good old acquaintance, no, more than that. I had a sense during these hours that I was walking in the footsteps of my Good Observer, which seemed to find confirmation in the fact that one time I was greeted by someone whose double I'd been as recently as the previous day: this person was weaving back and forth, sometimes bleating like a goat, sometimes grunting like a pig, swinging his arms like a threshing flail, and repeatedly darting into the road, where cars and trucks had to slam on their brakes, looking and sounding for all the world as if they were in a wide-screen movie—but the moment he caught sight of me, eyeing him quietly as I strode along: a greeting for me like no other, different from any ever shown in a film or ever to be seen in the future (before he outgrew his possession). By the way, like some others he'd come to a complete stop to greet me.

Several times after being greeted I received a casual hug from this or that stranger, male or female, and I returned the hug, though less spontaneously. And more than once the other person exclaimed, "There you are!" Just as all those who greeted me used the familiar form of "you," I used it all day with each of them.

Some cases of mistaken identity occurred. In quick

succession I was mistaken for a famous ski jumper, the piano player in the Grand Hotel bar, a celebrity lawyer, a football referee, a newspaper cartoonist, a gentleman farmer, an actor known for his cowboy roles, a funeral director (because of my black suit and white shirt?), even a notary (for the same reason?), if not a priest skipping out on his official duties—down with anything official!—(for the same reason?), a sailor on the way back to his ship (because of my wide-legged pants, fluttering in the wind?). And once I was mistaken for the last farmer in the region and in the entire land—and in that case the greeting and the hug were even heartier than usual because I, as that farmer, according to hearsay, the dominant form of news around there, had died weeks earlier. "How can this be, farmer—you're alive?! And look at how alive you are! Let me give you a hug!" And I? I let them persist in their error. And it may also be worth mentioning that a number of these apparent natives approached me, the stranger, for directions.

Others among those who greeted me as we passed each other realized afterward, as I could tell when I looked back and saw them stop and shake their heads, that they'd mistaken me for someone but couldn't for the life of them think who it might be. And others, the majority, I recall, greeted me only because I was me or, on that first day of my return "to my true nature," was the way I was, there—and then.

I can still hear some of the sayings the others directed at me as additional greetings: "Humans take revenge, not camels." — "Sometimes it helps to be patient." — "Heed your grandfather's example." — "Never stop following the Nile." — "Up and at the enemy!" — "Good works done in the open seldom do good." — "Who has two legs but seldom uses them?" — "Never use rotting strands to make a rope!" — "What the world needs now is a second verse." — "Come, let us weep together!" — "Keep at it till you drop." — "A mouth whose spittle is sweet." — "Leaving the house with bow in hand." — "Be not sorrowful." — "He who departs from the Decapolis will never return." — "Ride the chestnut mare." — "Buy yourself a quill pen." — "Not a soul at home." — "Ah, Mother." — "Oh, night rider." — "Dyin' ain't all" (that was in English).

What struck me most about all the greeters was this: despite being born into families that had lived here from time immemorial, they were in this land for only a brief sojourn. They'd been forced by a higher power, or some power or other, to go far, far away, and maybe by the next morning, or at any rate very soon, they'd be compelled to be gone again. Although no war was raging at the time, at least not in these parts, I couldn't help imagining that these people, younger as well as older ones, women as well as men, were in this land on leave, and even the one and only child, calling out piteously, "Wait for me!" when the troop of others had almost disappeared over the horizon, was here only thanks to a humanitarian operation known as "Respite from War." On call: back to the front with you all.

To the "front"? To the slaughter. And it was as if the only part I could see of those heading in that direction was their feet, walking, walking, walking, the feet of other "latter-day saints."

That, too, was an illusion. But this illusion, in contrast to good and lovely ones, didn't haunt me, nor did it trouble my mind; a moment later it had dissolved, become insubstantial. Remarkable nonetheless how later, for about an hour, starting in midafternoon, all kinds of chimeras (or what should I call them?) kept appearing as I made my way through this other land, each suddenly turning into its opposite, its antipode, as it were, and vice versa, and vice versa again.

A man was sitting on a boulder by the road, his back hunched as he cowered, motionless, facing away from everyone and everything, his feet rooted up to the ankles in the earth, and when I turned my head to look back at him, those feet were dangling high above the ground, swinging in midair, but when I looked a third time, it was no longer a game; instead the man was trying desperately to touch the ground from the boulder, but in vain—his legs were too short.

A very large woman, a giant in a police uniform, stomped into the concrete church, at once a shelter and a passageway, located on the side of yet another road. Her boots clacked, her holster creaked, and her handcuffs clanked. After first embodying the forces of law and order, without looking directly at me she threw herself on her knees so suddenly that the sound echoed through the nave, and then crawled, moving first her right knee, then her left, etc., to the altar. The uniformed giant knelt there in silence for a long time, then suddenly jumped up again and disappeared in a flash through the rear door.

After that someone exclaimed repeatedly, "I'm all alone!" the first time sobbing, the next time howling in triumph.

And when I walked backward myself for a short stretch, to get some rest (you read that right, I wrote "rest"), I saw my/our own land down on the plain on the far side of the lake as the other land, the entirely different land. (As I walked along backward, a driver pulled up next to me, thinking I was trying to hitch a ride.)

Another time I bent down along yet another road and scooped up a pencil that seemed to be nothing but a piece of wood but turned out to be a pencil after all—a thick, sturdy, old, half-weathered yet still usable carpenter's or cabinetmaker's pencil, and I murmured, "With pencil in hand / You're welcomed all through the land."

From some moment on and in some place no more illusions of any kind. And even before then, all day long it had been more than mere imagining, an actual certainty, that I was getting closer. Closer to whom? Getting closer. And it was equally clear that the individuals I met along the way, young ones as well as old, were "students," new or eternal beginners. — "Students from a driving school?" "Watch out, beginners!"? — Yes, watch out: beginners. Ah, my beginners, you of good will. —

A daydream? — Yes. But a daydream needn't be an illusion. After that hour in the afternoon this particular illusion at any rate helped me regain a firm footing. Obstacles blocked my path, one after the other: welcome, obstacles! And let's have another obstacle, please, and another—ah, the joy of obstacles. And persisting danger: one false step and I'd be done for, the story would be done for (what was it that was said in the end of that hero, the survivor of a different story, a very old one, from yet another land: "He lived that he might tell the tale"?)

And then again how strange, truly "worth telling," that I, in awareness of the danger, succeeded as a pitcher, landing every pitch, at whatever, with whatever, yet without a gong or a bell sounding to mark the hits: gentle pitches, the gentlest possible. Thank you, danger.

And then came the moment when I lacked literally everything that day, and then suddenly lacked nothing, nothing at all. All that counted: I'm somewhere else. And: anywhere but home. Never to go home again!

One time, not far from my destination in the Decapolis, I missed by a hair gambling away that whole day in the other land, and not that alone. I forgot one of the rules, and not the most insignificant one: as I walked along the road I started keeping my eyes peeled for treasure. It happened out of carelessness or who knows why, a relapse to a phase in childhood when I'd thought I was cut out to be a treasure hunter, and was also convinced I'd find some treasure, though without having the slightest notion of what it might be.

At the last moment I recognized the peril: I was at risk of being disqualified. In a panic I pleaded, if not prayed, for an image spied out of the corner of my eye that would save me. There was one, a "trail" of apple cores, most of them almost completely consumed, seeds and all, varieties I could still recognize even after years of madness, each one distinct from the others. But it wasn't this image that got me back into the game but, unexpectedly, and above all irrevocably, the images that now, at this very moment, wafted toward me as fleetingly as shooting stars, from far outside and deep within me, images of all the places where I'd once spent time, or which I'd merely passed through without consciously registering anything, let alone storing it in my memory; not even the place as a place with a name, a place name, had meant anything to me; only now, as a shooting image, did it receive a name and become a place, my place, one of my places. And it was only images like these that came to my aid: treasures not to be found by scanning the ground. No more treasure hunting, ever.

After that no more rules, either. I took shortcuts—earlier frowned upon—and likewise took long ways around, and without exception lovely ones. More and more I didn't keep to the straight and narrow, for instance when I traced the winding ribbons of tar along the edge of the road. And as I did so, the message came winging toward me from all the horizons: "He who rejoiceth in the day rejoiceth in the world."

And then a final festive-day stretch, on which I celebrated my birthday (the one on my birth certificate? Does it matter?). It was also the only time during that day when I read something (or, after years of madness and sadness with not a single word read consciously, began to read anew), if only—again wafted toward me, though not in the same way as the images—a yellowed scrap or passage torn out of a centuries-old dictionary of ancient Greek, with a sentence fragment that I joyfully decoded word by word and accepted as my birthday present: "He who rubs against many door posts scrapes his shoulders." Or "abrades"?

After that, appropriately for this kind of birthday celebration, came the last words of an old woman lying in the grass by the side of a road and about to die. People were clustered around her, obviously strangers, of whom one or two were bending over her, and as I took a step closer, the old woman gazed around the circle, her eyes glowing, and declared, in a voice as full of vitality as could be, "I love you all."

And then, a mile or a verst farther on, I myself felt ready to die on this special birthday. I even stopped in my tracks and waited. I sat down on a curbstone, perhaps a milestone from long ago, and waited. Head tilted skyward. Head bent earthward, to the pavement, to my shoes. For a fraction of a second I felt death inside me, gathering itself for a somersault. But when nothing happened I took a deep breath and went on my way, refreshed.

Children's voices a long way off, as if coming from the treetops, if not from the heavens. A preacher on the side of the road, his voice weak, seemingly failing him, but carrying all the farther, out into the land. (And what was he preaching? He was preaching.) And twined around the sign announcing the next town's name a wild apple tree, its two or three fruits, very small, already picked and tasted: bitterness of bitternesses, bitterness as medicine. The breeze generated by my walking putting its arm around my waist, the sensation lingering long afterward.

With my arrival in the center of the former Decapolis: the culmination of the festive stretches I'd walked that day. In their place a different festivity, noticeable at first only to me and then to this person or that, a clandestine festivity yet all the more ubiquitous. Furthermore, all the centers of the Decapolis—which it still called itself, though the ten cities were long gone—were at the same time peripheries, as the peripheries in turn constituted centers. So the name of the center in question doesn't matter? Given the aforementioned festive atmosphere, and for this story of mine, perhaps it does matter for a change: Kursi, which translates to throne.

Remnants of a stone staircase: all that's left of the *kursi* from two thousand years ago. Otherwise almost exclusively buildings from the most recent, current, and, why not?, future times; likewise the furniture and fixtures the same as in the other land, run-of-the-mill.

And yet, and yet . . . And on that evening the distinctiveness resulted not merely from the town's name.

It matched my festive mood that after all my years of eating alone, living literally from hand to mouth, for the first time I now dined with others at a common table. The others taking part in the festive occasion: chance acquaintances, or not chance after all—as I'd sensed immediately when I met them while exploring the city, and that proved to be the case that night. I'd made the acquaintance of one of them while playing table football, of the second in front of a jukebox. And the third was a very young policeman—another person from the forces of law and order—who, newly arrived in the city, had lost his way and took me for someone familiar with the place (see above) and then stuck to my heels. We formed a small group, strangers to each other, and despite quietly maintaining our strangerhood, were of one mind.

That would have been the moment, would have been the hour, for telling these strangers in the other land my story, as I'd been instructed. And instead until midnight they told me their stories, unbidden and not interrupted by a single question from me. They held nothing back, spoke trustingly, solemnly. But these stories of theirs turn up in a different book, can be read, transformed, in other books—yes, you guessed right, mine from later years, no longer on the subject of espaliered fruit trees.

And that was all I'd hoped for. As I took in these

strangers' stories and their manner of telling them, I knew: "This is it. And this is how it is. And only this is it. And this is only how it is." And while we dined, chatted, raised our glasses, and celebrated, it was as if we were also keeping house. Without the "as if." We were keeping house. On a glass off to one side, in partial darkness, I saw the imprint of my future sweetheart's lips shimmering. Coincidences? Not coincidences? And what if it was—only—a coincidence: let a coincidence like that play its role.

Hoping for nothing more? Suddenly I felt like dancing. That's hardly ever happened to me, and maybe that evening in Kursi was the very first time; in the past, hadn't I always needed to be pressured to dance?

And long after midnight I met my future bride in a dance hall, for real; it couldn't have been more real. She took me by surprise, and I took her by surprise; we surprised each other. As I remember it, she greeted me with "Hey there, weirdo!" and I greeted her the same way, though neither of us said a word. But we silently invented a dance that in later years I called the "Catch Me If You Can" dance (and that name should be kept). This is how it went: one of us would slip away or simply dance off among the other dancers, and the partner would have to catch up.

At one point I had the impression that a bystander was laughing at me. But he was merely smiling at the buzzard's feather I'd picked up along the way and stuck in my hair, forgetting it was there. When I removed it, my future bride put it back. Remembering that, I think I can feel rice being tossed at us.

The years that followed were harmonious. I rejoiced in every day and felt sure that was my true nature. Above all I was a thoroughly sociable being, effective in whatever I undertook or let be, in living and letting live, perhaps more in the latter: disarming; and "Let-Liver" became a sort of nickname. My wife sometimes remarked, and not entirely in jest, that I'd have made a good politician, the ideal one, modeling a new politics, putting it into practice, of a sort sorely needed nowadays. True: "No more divisiveness; an end to this chronic partisanship; we should all get along, make common cause!" And that conviction could be read in my face, and not only there.

But how does it happen that I now also see the faces of my children before me, as over the years they would suddenly, unexpectedly, stare at me, though not often—at the least propitious moments, so to speak— but their wide eyes would show such fear and, worse still, growing distrust, a loss of trust and not only in me, their father. Threefold fear and horror: of and at me, for me, and of and at themselves, my children—their horror and fear were legion, never to be made right.

3

Last night I dreamed that I was back in my niche in the old graveyard on the steppe. It had become a shed, or merely one wall made of rough planks. Hanging on the wall was a mirror, a splendid one, looking freshly polished. When I stepped up to it, I wasn't merely startled; I was overcome with horror: a stranger stared out at me, bearing not the slightest resemblance to me, as unfamiliar as is possible only in a dream. But with my first blink the horror changed to astonishment, and the astonishment gave way to trust. No trace of burning eyes, hair on end, flared nostrils. A man both weary and gentle gazed out at me, from whose lips I read, "Be not afraid." Behind him in the mirror I saw a glow like that of unknown stellar and planetary systems in the universe.

For a dream interval neither of us spoke, the only sound the wind whistling in a lone tree on the steppe, like whispering. Then came lip-reading, which felt to me like being poked, sentence after sentence, poke after poke, as I had been poked one time, while swimming in a mountain river, by the lips, the mouth of a trout, poked in the backs of my knees, ever so delicately, a project for peace if ever there was one: "A creature of society, that's all well and good. But aren't you also a fundamentally different creature, at once poorer and much richer? And well and good, too, your harmoniousness, your harmonies when it comes to 'snuggling into the curve of being,' 'letting existence bubble,' in 'being, joy materialized.' But where's the oppositional element, what have you done with the resistance that's integral to your nature, the nonsociable part that resists being socialized and is occasionally even hostile to society? Yes, what's happened to the resistance that's not just integral to your nature but forms its very core, and fortunately so, and not for you alone!? It may be that this resistance, the ineradicable oppositional element in you, is a sickness, but that sickness is also healthful and has curative powers, and, also fortunately, not for you alone. Without resistance, without that sickness, and without that good fortune, nothing can take shape. Without them nothing but ordinary being, being there, and eternally soulless existence. Taking shape! Taking shape! Something's going on with me, with you! Exciting things are happening with you and me—let them happen! Yes, you exist, and fortunately for us again, 'the two of us,' and on this foundation, whether we're chosen or condemned to it, we'll build our castles in the air. We, you as well as me, will build those castles to the end of our days. We, you as well as me, never wanted to build anything, certainly nothing solid, nothing massive. Nothing that would add mass to our poor planet, already being built up to death! But those castles in the air of ours: they're different. A mixed-up mess? Yes, back to the mixed-up mess with us. And write that on a slip of paper and sew it into your garment, or stick it up your ass. Maelstrom of beats, caravan route from a different time. Salt sprinkled into the book of our lives, the lives of us all!"

And then the face of the stranger in the mirror revealed something familiar, something with which I was intimately acquainted: amid all the gray, brown, and already white hairs in his beard were two or three that were red and had remained that way, as red as on the first day, red with a touch of hornet's yellow, sticking out at me from the mirror like quills, dangerous, poisonous ones. But that was deceptive: with those reddish-yellow beard tips, multiplied as if specifically for the dream, what I had before me was a human face, plain and simple.

Involuntarily, as if whisked away from the mirror, I gave myself a hug, wrapped my arms around myself in the far corner of the abandoned graveyard, which felt as though it had sunk beneath the waves. It was a moonlit night, and atop the gravestones, likewise multiplied as if specifically for the dream and rendered much taller, without inscriptions, wiped clean of inscriptions, perched birds, sleeping in migratory thousands and forming a skyline. Rejoicing filled me; and a lust for adventure.

I looked over my shoulder into a blackness to end all blackness, blackness such as occurs only in dreams, and uttered a war cry—not meant as such—or perhaps meant as such after all?—which I heard in my sleep as inarticulate squawking, and then I called into the void, clearly this time: "Are you there, all of you?"

—Summer and fall 2020